BYLINES AND BLOODSUCKERS

A RAVENS HOLLOW INVESTIGATION PREQUEL

ELLA STONE

PAPER CAT PUBLISHER

ALSO BY ELLA STONE

The Dark Creatures Saga

Dark Creatures

Dark Destiny

Dark Deception

Dark Redemption

Dark Reckoning

The Bloodsuckers Blog Trilogy

Life Sucks

Love Bites

Lost Souls

The Ravens Hollow Investigations

Bylines and Bloodsuckers

Fangs and Front Pages

Hexes and Headlines

Demons and Deadlines

BY ELLA STONE & HEATHER G HARRIS

The Witchlight Magical Mysteries

Secrets of the Frostbound Cottage

Secrets of the Forgotten Heir

Secrets of the Deadly Nightshades

Secrets of the Eternal Flame

This story is a work of fiction. All names, characters, organisations, places, events and incidents are products of the author's imagination or are used fictitiously. Any resemblance to any persons, alive or dead, events or locals is entirely coincidental.

Paper Cat Publishing

ISBN: 978-1-915346-56-8

Edited by Karen Holmes
Cover by Christian Bentulan

For Sammy, whose been there forever,

CHAPTER
ONE

'No? You're saying *no*?'

My jaw hung loose as I stared at my boss. Surely I'd misheard her; either that or she was doing a very poor job of being a comedian, because there was no way she could seriously be saying no to this.

But she had said no. And then she said it again to reinforce the point. 'That's right, Elodie, I'm saying no. I don't want you to investigate this.' She pushed the envelope full of papers back across the desk towards me.

Down by my feet, Wilbur yawned widely. The black-and-white spaniel wasn't mine, but he attached himself to my heels whenever his owner was in a meeting. He'd been fast asleep in the comfy bed I had set up for him in my office, and it was clear he wanted to get back to it, but there was no way I was leaving this room until I had answers.

'Why?' It was the only word rolling over and over in my head. I'd thought Donna would jump on the story. As far as investigative journalism went, this was a scoop in the making and I was so close to cracking it. That was why I'd come to her now with the evidence, expecting her to give me the go ahead to bring others onto the team. Instead, she wanted to shut it down.

'Why the hell would you not want me looking into it?' I demanded.

'Because I don't think there's a story,' Donna replied. She wasn't looking at me but tapping away on her computer instead. Maybe she just wanted to avoid my scowl? But no, Donna never tapped away at her computer when she was talking to someone; she always gave them her full attention. That was what made her a great editor-in-chief and a damn good friend. Normally.

This was not normal. So maybe it was a prank?

'You're joking, right?' I said. 'There's a massive story. Maybe you missed it in my notes. Let me show you—' I reached for the manilla envelope but she placed her hand firmly on it and stopped me pushing it back towards her.

'I read it properly, Elodie. I promise you whatever you think is happening here is all conjecture. You're jumping to conclusions. I'm not letting you throw yourself down this rabbit hole to find there's nothing at the bottom of it. There are more important stories you could be working on right now – like that tip we got about the politician who's been embezzling. '

I threw up my hands in frustration. 'Politicians are always embezzling funds. That's not a story – it would only be a story if we actually found an *honest* MP. And anyway, a lot of good stories start with a hunch and it's often a lot smaller than this one.'

Donna breathed in deeply and finally turned her attention from her screen to me.

'If you want something different, you could always do a piece on the new sport centre in Clapham where they seem to have cut corners on the building work. Apparently several people have received suction burns from using the toilets near the swimming pool. That's not the type of story that comes along every week, and it would make use of your sports' expertise.'

At any other time the idea of someone getting a suction burn from a toilet bowl would have warranted deeper thought, but it wasn't going to distract me now. 'Sports' expertise?' I echoed. 'Now you have to be taking the mick.'

At a paper as big as *The Sentinel*, there were teams of journalists, including sports ones, meaning there was a whole list of people better suited to that investigation than me. My sports' expertise started and ended with throwing javelins for my university, so unless readers wanted to know whether a Finnish or Fork Grip had been used to flush the offending toilets, then I didn't think I was her person. And even if they did, what she was asking me to do was not investigative journalism. Unlike the story I'd just placed on her desk.

'People are going missing, Donna,' I persisted. 'That's something that deserves our attention. Look.' I yanked the envelope out from under her hand and pulled out one of the pages. 'Every month for the last *thirteen* months, people have been disappearing and their last sightings are always around here.'

'People are always going missing. This is London,' Donna sighed.

'Yes, people go missing all the time – randomly. But not like this. Three people a month, always from South London. Always around the seventh of the month. And that's not the only common factor. Every victim has been between the ages of thirty-nine and sixty. That's not the normal demographic for missing people, it's decades over.'

'Have you looked at the divorce rate in that area of London? Maybe they're just people who are—'

'Why are you not listening to me, Donna?' I clenched my hands, willing myself to stay calm, but it was hard. I was right about this, I knew I was. I had a lead on a massive story and Donna wasn't *listening*.

I wasn't just angry – I was bloody confused.

Donna had been nothing but supportive towards me since I'd started work at *The Sentinel* almost a decade ago. Back then I'd been a staff writer and she'd been lower down the ladder, as well. Her role when we'd first met was as an online editor, though she'd made it very clear the position was only the first rung and I had loved her certainty.

We'd struck up a friendship straight away and she was central in giving me the courage to fight my way up the company ladder too, encouraging me to follow up leads that other people would have dismissed. Leads like this one, which was why I was continuing to stress my point.

If she wanted me out of her office, she'd have to drag me out by my hair. And I'd seen that woman at CrossFit: she had the upper body strength of an anaemic woodlouse.

'I've pinpointed the locations.' I pulled out a map and tapped on an area of forest to the north-east of London. 'I'm certain this is the central point, Sydenham Hill Wood. If I'm right, there'll be another kidnapping soon – tomorrow, actually.'

With another loud sigh, Donna folded her arms and sat back in her swivel chair. 'Elodie, I don't mean to sound cruel, but you have to admit that you don't always think clearly when it comes to missing people.'

A muscle ticked along my jaw as I fought back the urge to yell.

'My mother has nothing to do with this.' I was impressed with how I kept my voice measured, given the anger rolling through me. 'And she didn't go missing. She left us. Left us and disappeared without a trace. That is *not* the same thing.'

The way Donna's lips pursed told me she disagreed, but I didn't care. The fact I hadn't seen my mother, Maria, in twenty years wasn't because she'd gone missing, but because she'd found being a parent and wife too much effort, and she'd decided a family holiday to the Seychelles was the best time to write us a letter saying she was leaving. No, this story was definitely not about my mother. It was about people going missing. People who actually needed help.

'Regardless,' Donna said after a pause. 'I do *not* want

you following this up.' There was no room for negotiation in her voice. 'If what you're saying is true, and people—'

'Donna you—'

'I'm not done,' she said sharply. 'If people were going missing from there, the police would be onto it. It's just pure speculation and we don't do that in our line of work.'

'It's only pure speculation because I haven't gone there to look for the evidence,' I said. 'In a week's time, it won't be speculation because I'll have caught the damned people who are doing this.'

'That is not your job. Your job is reporting. This is *non-negotiable*, Elodie. You are to drop all thoughts about this story because there *is* no story. Do you understand?'

I ground my back teeth together.

She obviously read my silence as defiance which, of course, it was. 'Put it this way. If you don't follow my orders and drop this, I'll have to seriously consider whether or not you're ready for that promotion you just applied for.'

Her words were like a punch to my stomach. She had to be joking. Didn't she?

Heat prickled behind my eyes. I had never cried at work, not once, but maybe it was because this was different. Donna knew there was nobody at the paper more deserving of the role of executive editor. I had given this paper my *everything* – three years ago, I'd actually skipped out on my own engagement party early when I'd got a lead.

Thankfully, my fiancé Andy had been perfectly happy to cut the event short and head home for a cup of Ovaltine and an episode of some superhero show while the party carried on without us. He'd already made several comments about how he thought the venue had misjudged the capacity it could hold, not to mention the noise level in the enclosed space and the fact that the guests – *our* guests – had helped themselves to the canapés that had been set aside for him and his IBS.

From across the desk, Donna stared hard at me. 'I'm sorry, Elodie, really I am. But as my best friend and my employee, you'll have to trust me. In the long run, I'm sure you'll see I'm right.'

I couldn't believe she had pulled the best-friend card on me. That really was the last straw. Frustration rattled through me and, with a noise that sounded surprisingly animal-like, I snatched the envelope from the table.

'If *The Telegraph* scoops this, you're gonna need to find yourself another journalist,' I said, before marching out and slamming the door behind me.

Hot tears welled in my eyes as I marched back to my office with Wilbur at my side. I wasn't just angry that Donna didn't want what was obviously a killer story; it was the way she'd tried to leverage our friendship to make me drop it. My stomach roiled. Maybe I didn't know my best friend as well as I thought I did. Either way, I could probably kiss that promotion goodbye.

CHAPTER TWO

'You've always told me Donna knows what she's doing,' Andy said that night as he handed me a plate of unseasoned chicken, white rice and boiled carrots. 'Although I've had my doubts.'

It was the third night in a row that we'd eaten that same meal, but Andy's IBS had been playing up and when he was feeling delicate even the *smell* of spices had him pulling faces and clutching his belly. The last thing I could deal with was his groaning as he sat on the sofa watching television. Of course, maybe if we were the type of couple who enjoyed a bit of adventurous sexy time, groaning on the sofa wouldn't always be a bad thing. But we didn't. Ever.

'She has. She does,' I agreed, tapping my fingers repeatedly on the table. 'Which is why this is so confusing. I spoke to other people at the desk and they all seem to think it's a great idea.'

'Do you want me to say something to her?'

I gritted my teeth. Andy was an intelligent man, one of those people who was annoyingly good at most things he tried, which sometimes made him think he had the right to stick his nose in where it wasn't wanted.

And he knew Donna well.

I'd met him only a month or so after starting at *The Sentinel*, and that was part of the problem; he felt he'd come up the ranks with us despite his own job being in finance, and that could lead to some severe cases of mansplaining. Mostly I could tune them out the way someone would do when they worked in an office with an overly loud fridge, or a colleague who insisted on telling them about their weekend plans every Friday even though they did the same thing every weekend.

Other people, like Donna, weren't so adept at ignoring Andy's mansplaining sessions. As such, those two got on like a coeliac and a stone-fired bloomer loaf.

I wasn't oblivious to the fact that Donna thought Andy wasn't the ideal match for me. Maybe it was because she knew that I'd dive into the spiciest curry when I was out for dinner with her, or maybe it was because his idea of being daring was to leave the washing unfolded in the basket overnight so he could watch another episode of his favourite show.

Andy didn't want to travel like I did – who knew what nasties would be lurking in foreign food? He didn't want children, although admittedly I'd never been a hundred percent sure about having them either. He insisted that any spare cash at the end of the month went straight into the pension he'd started the minute he'd got his first job.

True, he wasn't the most romantic or inspiring guy, but that was exactly why I felt so comfortable with him: he was reliable.

Sure, the way my mother had abandoned my father and me, had probably influenced why I'd ended up with someone like Andy, but it wasn't the only reason.

As an investigative journalist, I never knew where the day would take me. My working life was full of spur-of-the-moment decisions, adrenaline rushes followed by massive crashes, or highs that lasted just a few days before I sought the next one. The last thing I needed was that kind of unpredictability in a relationship.

Did Andy set my world alight? No. Did he provide even the slightest smouldering spark that meant after a couple of glasses of wine, I'd find myself overcome with lust? That would be a no, too.

But I did know that each night after a hectic day at work I'd come home to the bed made, no socks on the floor, the toilet seat down (not to mention wiped with unscented antibacterial spray), and no video games or television blaring in the middle of the night when I wanted to sleep. And there were advantages to being with a guy who kept a list of everything in the food cupboard; in all the time we'd been living together, we'd never run out of ground coriander or smoked paprika. Not that I could remember using them, but hey.

Still, I knew Donna wouldn't take kindly to Andy making suggestions about how to run her massively successful newspaper.

'No, of course not,' I said. 'It's fine.'

Sensing the need to change the subject – for both of us – he spoke again. ‘ I thought you said those succulents you bought were non-flowering,’ he said. ‘The ones in the bathroom.’

‘They should be. Or at least that’s what the person at the garden centre told me. Not when they’re kept indoors, anyway.’

‘Well, they were wrong. There are dozens of flowers on them. It’s just like that cactus you bought a couple of months ago – and you know how my skin can react to pollen. When we moved in together, I only agreed to you having your plants if they didn’t flower. I think you need to rethink, maybe take a few more to the office. It’s bad enough that the council won’t chop down that cherry tree on the road. You’d think they’d actually want to listen to their constituents, particularly when it’s a health issue.’

Given that the health issue Andy was talking about was sore eyes, a runny nose and an itchy skin that I swear only itched because he started scratching himself every time he saw a pollen-filled stamen, I was pretty sure that the council had far bigger problems to deal with.

He was right about the succulents being in flower, though. I’d noticed them before I’d left for work that morning and had planned to move them before he spotted the pretty blossoms. Unfortunately, with all the drama over Donna and my story, I’d not had chance. Hence I’d been busted.

It was weird that they’d flowered so quickly. Knowing that the garden centre had been wrong before, I’d checked the varieties online, and even then I’d picked the sickliest specimens in the hope that they'd take longer to flower. I also knew that bringing them back to full health would give me a deep sense of satisfaction. I didn't have green thumbs, I had green hands – the full five fingers, not to mention palms and all the way up to my wrist. I loved my plants. And as for taking more to work, my office was so full of plants it had earned the nickname 'the jungle'.

'Oh, talking about people at the paper,' I said, shifting the conversation again, 'I spoke to Mitchell today. He brought his doodle into work.'

Andy arched an eyebrow. 'A doodle?'

'It's a dachshund-cross-poodle. They're tiny – and – hypoallergenic. One of those would probably cause even fewer problems than the plants.'

Lots of people brought their dogs to the newsroom; that helped me get my daily fix of canine companionship but it also meant I got first-hand experience of what I was missing. My desperate love of animals was well known and I'd formed some firm furry friendships, the closest of which was definitely Wilbur.

His owner, Sonia, wrote the agony-aunt column, and I'd known Wilbur since he was a puppy. He was without doubt my favourite office dog and not only because he loved having his long fur intricately plaited; he also insisted on showing new dogs around the office. Actually, that probably was my favourite thing: Wilbur would take the newcomers to each room, including mine, then linger in the kitchen until someone brought down the treat jar to make sure that the new addition knew where the snacks were kept.

Wilbur always slept under my desk when Sonia had to nip out and couldn't take him, and at least once a week I took him for his lunchtime walk so she could hit her deadlines. Countless times over the years she'd suggested I borrow Wilbur overnight so that Andy could see just how calming a dog could be – and coming from a spaniel owner that was saying something. But I knew there was no chance Andy would say yes, so I hadn't even bothered raising the question.

I'd hoped a tiny, hypoallergenic doodle might at least open up a conversation about pets, but from the way he groaned and rolled his eyes I knew I'd set my hopes a little high.

'Elodie, you *know* my allergies won't stand a dog, not even one of those hypoallergenic ones. Besides, I'm not the type of man who walks around with a dog called a doodle. It's just not happening. It's no pets for me – and no flowers. Unless, of course, you'd rather exchange your Andy-Pandy for a stray dog and a monthly subscription to the local florist?'

Andy-Pandy: I didn't know who had made up the cloying nickname but it sure as hell wasn't me.

Obviously I wasn't going to ruin a perfectly reasonable relationship for the sake of getting a dog. Andy and I had been together for eight years and for the last three I'd been wearing a small diamond ring on my left hand, though we hadn't fixed a wedding date. Andy seemed to think that some point in the next decade sounded reasonable.

'While we're on the topic of animals,' he said, continuing a conversation I'd assumed was over, 'we got another four of those letters through the post last week.'

'Letters?' I played ignorant as I had about the succulents, acting like I had no idea what he was talking about even though I did.

'From the animal charities?' he pressed. 'There were two the week before, all asking for money obviously. Orangutangs, whales – it's not like you're going to see any of these animals you're helping. There was even one asking for money to help kittens. I mean really, Elodie? *Kittens*? They're not even endangered.'

'I think it's because—'

Before I could continue, he carried on. 'We agreed we'd support your bleeding-heart charities for a year. Any more than that and it's digging into our pension.'

'I know,' I said, grateful he didn't know just how many coins I dropped into charity workers' buckets in the street. Or how many more of those direct debit forms were stashed at the bottom of my underwear drawer. 'It's just that last year's has come to an end so I'm thinking about which I should sponsor next.'

'Well, pick a cheap one. You know that hardly any of the money goes to the good causes – it's all used up in admin, meaning you're basically paying for the CEO's whisky supply. Speaking of which, I'm going out tomorrow night.' He shuddered. 'For dinner.'

The way he said 'dinner' was how a normal person spoke about filling in a tax return. Although knowing Andy, he'd probably prefer to deal with the tax than eat out.

'How come?'

He groaned. 'A thank you from the shareholders, some of whom will be there. Apparently the staff who don't show up get smaller bonuses. It'll be dull, and there'll be nothing I can eat. I'd much rather be here with you.'

Comments like that reminded me why I was happy with Andy and our sheltered life. After all, given how few people he liked it had to be a massive compliment that I was the person he wanted to spend the rest of his life with.

I looked down at the plate in front of me. If Andy was out of the house, I wouldn't feel guilty about getting a takeaway, something spicy like Thai or Vietnamese. I'd have to make sure I put all the rubbish in the outside bins; sometimes just the smell was enough to set off his stomach.

'Any idea what time you'll be back?' I asked.

'They like to go for drinks afterwards so they probably won't leave until closing time, which is ridiculous. But we have to do what we have to do. That's how jobs work. By *networking*.' He winced at the word.

'Yes. Yes of course,' I said, though I was no longer really listening.

It was as if a dodgy lightbulb had finally found a connection and switched on in my head. Andy was right: you had to do what you had to do because that was how jobs worked.

I felt a flutter of excitement deep in my stomach. I wouldn't be getting a take-away tomorrow after all; I'd be following my hunch because I was a damn good investigative journalist and I was going to prove it. I was going to do my job, and finish this case, whether Donna wanted me to or not.

Better to ask for forgiveness, than permission, right? Donna would totally forgive me when I'd uncovered a kidnapping ring. In fact, not only would she forgive me, she'd be grovelling for *my* forgiveness.

It was a good thing Andy was going out because it looked like I had a stakeout to plan.

CHAPTER
THREE

It had been a while since I'd done a stakeout, and because this one was technically unsanctioned my tension levels were high. 'Nervcitement', that's what I called it when excitement mingled with nerves to a point where I had a fairly good idea what Andy's stomach would feel like after a hefty dose of Sriracha.

Normally, I'd have taken someone with me on a trip like this, such as a photographer with one of those crazy zoom-lens cameras or a newbie intern hoping to get their name on a byline. But Donna couldn't have been firmer in telling me to stay away, and the last thing I wanted to do was derail some new hire's career before it had even started, even if it gave them a break from fetching everyone tea and coffee while being yelled at for things that were absolutely not their fault. And as for the photographers? They answered to Donna, not me, and I couldn't risk them letting slip to her where we were going.

Anyway, going alone meant that when I finally busted

these crooks, all the credit would be mine. I could see it now: awards would be coming my way, and not just journalism ones.

If I was right, I was going to break open a whole ring of traffickers – traffickers that specialised in people over forty. Clearly there was some kind of niche market there and, while I didn't know what it was yet, I would sure as hell find out. Find the culprits, bust them and reap the rewards. When I had this gang behind bars, the accolades would come. Television interviews, perhaps; my name as a headline and not just the byline.

I could see it all: the letters of thanks and the grateful gifts – which mostly consisted of designer shoes, or expenses-paid holidays that I could take Andy on without him worrying about his bloody pension pot. This would be the start of a whole new chapter in my life. I just had to catch the arseholes first.

Besides, not being able to take another person with me didn't mean I had to go on my own.

'I'm so glad Andy's coming around to the idea of having a dog,' Sonia said as she handed me Wilbur's lead outside the newsroom.

'I wanted to strike while the iron is hot,' I said. A flicker of guilt sparked within me for lying to my colleague, especially when she'd agreed with less than a day's notice to let me borrow her furry friend. 'That's why I messaged last night.'

'Oh I get it,' she said. 'Honestly, it's completely fine. Wilbur's not had much of a walk today – work took over. The longer you can give him tonight, the better.'

'A long walk?' I couldn't stop the smile rising on my lips. 'I don't think that's going to be a problem.'

From my investigation so far, I had located Sydenham Hill Wood as the epicentre of the area that the missing people came from. While it helped to have an area on which to focus my search, it wasn't a pinpoint location because the patch of greenery on the outskirts of London was twenty-five acres of woodland. It was safe to say that Wilbur would get his long walk.

'Thanks for this, boy,' I said as he jumped into my car. 'I know – I'm a big brave journalist who needs a friend's dog to go on a stakeout in a wood. But how about this? You help me with this and we'll get the other type of "steak out" for dinner.'

Wilbur's tail beat enthusiastically against the seat, though that was probably due to my use of the 'd' word rather than anything else. Aware that we had a long night ahead of us, and that Wilbur already had expectations of food, I filled his bowl with the biscuits Sonia had given me and fed him in the back of the car. Andy would pass out if he found out what I was doing – but hey, what he didn't know couldn't hurt him.

The one non-negotiable item I took with me on every trip was a small can of defence spray. Pepper spray was banned in the UK, and this was my alternative. I couldn't comment on its effectiveness because I'd never had to use it before, but considering it dyed the victim a deep red colour I couldn't imagine it would be too pleasant if I sprayed it in their face.

The sun was disappearing below the horizon as we

entered the woods and most people were going in the opposite direction, heading home for the night. After all, who would willingly go into a wood with Victorian ruins and a disused train line after dark?

Me. That was who.

It was one of those nights when the cloud cover was so dense it was impossible to believe there were any stars beyond it. The lack of light only added to the nervousness bubbling through me.

'Bringing you was a good idea,' I said to Wilbur. 'And don't worry, I won't let anything happen to you. You are my number one priority – you, and saving these people, obviously.' He was already busy sniffing the ground.

I hadn't worked out what I'd do with him after we'd finished here, but I wasn't anticipating going home. By the time the police arrived and I'd given my statement, it would be time to get him his steak and hand him back to Sonia. And if I did have to take him back to Andy, surely there was no way he could be mad; without Wilbur by my side, I might not have had the guts to break the biggest story of my career.

'You know, you'll probably get a medal for this too,' I said. 'And maybe a lifetime's supply of bones. That would be good, wouldn't it? I'll tell you what, even if no one else gets you them, I will.'

Soon it was just the two of us alone with the sounds of the forest. Suddenly I was even more nervy, and the noise made by some small creature scuttling in the undergrowth made me almost jump out of my skin.

For the most part, Wilbur was incredibly stealthy,

though every now and then he sniffed something that made him pull at his lead and made my pulse rocket.

The shrill ringing of my phone sent my heart so far up my throat that I nearly choked. 'Shit,' I muttered, cursing my rookie mistake. What kind of idiot on a stakeout in a quiet forest left their phone on full volume? Me, apparently.

Wanting to silence it as quickly as possible, I cut the call. Immediately, a message buzzed through. Donna.

Hey, wondered if you wanted to catch up for a quiet drink tonight? I saw Andy. He said he was going for dinner.

Crap. That meant I couldn't use *having a quiet night in with the fiancé* as an excuse for declining.

Thanks, but I'm having an early night, I replied, still trying to keep my eyes on my surroundings in case someone was about to pounce on me from behind. *Already in the bath.*

Three dots appeared and I waited for her response, but the moment stretched as if she were struggling to find the right words. Considering how long it was taking her to type, I expected more than the three words that finally pinged through: *Okay. Have fun.*

I read the message multiple times, wondering if it had any deeper significance. It just didn't sound like Donna; usually she grabbed any chance that I was free of Andy to get me out with her and Jules. Then again, she'd said 'a quiet drink'. When the three of us socialised, it usually turned into the sort of raucous night where you came home with a stuffed parrot, a sharpie tattoo and several flights booked to places you'd never heard of.

Perhaps Donna had just decided it wasn't worth the hangover.

Shaking off the feeling of uncertainty, I pocketed my phone – only for everything to suddenly get a lot darker than it had been before.

Something swooped over my head – an owl, perhaps? While I ducked and muttered something under my breath, Wilbur stood deathly still. As I reached down to stroke his fur and reassure him that everything was alright, I realised what had caused his reaction.

He'd heard something and this time, it was definitely *not* an animal because they were talking.

'I'm not sure if we've got this right,' a man said. 'I thought they were meant to meet us by now.'

My heart skittered in my chest. Men skulking in the wood after dark? That had immense kidnapper potential. I just had to make sure they didn't spot me skulking too.

'Really? At this hour?' another man responded, his voice weighted with sarcasm. 'Obviously, you haven't done your research, Marcus.'

'Of course I've done my research, Cameron,' the first voice snapped back. 'I wouldn't be here if I hadn't.'

'Boys, will you please stop it?' This time it was the voice of a long-suffering woman. She spoke too quietly for me to catch her next words.

I strained to listen as I picked up my pace and headed in their direction. After a minute or two, I heard them again. Whilst their whispering was still too low to make out any words, their feet were clumping loudly through the undergrowth. Stealth was not their strongest suit.

Judging by their voices, they were middle aged – just like the missing people.

'We'll wait here,' the one called Cameron spoke again. There was something about his tone that reminded me of the men I'd met in the city with their smart shoes and leather briefcases. He wasn't asking their opinion, he was telling them.

A moment later the crunching of leaves stopped, from which I assumed they'd all agreed with his decision. As they fell silent, my heart drummed against my ribcage.

'Okay, boy,' I whispered to Wilbur. 'Time to get comfy.' They were planning on waiting, so that's what I would do, too.

The only difference was that, unlike them, I had no idea what I was waiting for.

CHAPTER FOUR

Over the next couple of hours, Wilbur and I moved slowly to get as close to the group as we could. I watched every footstep as I tried to make as little noise as possible, but I could only manage a few steps at a time because I didn't want to attract their attention. Neither did I want to move in the wrong direction.

The third reason we moved so slowly was Wilbur's obsession with picking up sticks. Every few paces, his tail started wagging at an uncontrollable speed and his head disappeared into the leaf litter, only for him to reappear with a broken branch in his jaw. He'd walk on happily for a few minutes, head up and proud as punch at his new find, then sniff, stop in his tracks, discard the treasured item and pick up a new one. I had never before realised how fickle a canine's love could be.

Irritating as it could have been, Wilbur's constant stop-start approach helped me keep my footing on the constantly changing terrain. There was no chance I could risk using my phone torch, and while the clouds occasionally shifted to offer the briefest glimpse of the full moon hiding behind them, there was nowhere near enough light to see by.

Thankfully, every now and then one of the three people tried to strike up a conversation. It was usually Marcus and he was almost immediately shut down by Cameron, but it was enough for me to check my bearings and take another step toward them,

'Do you think the pain will be horrendous?' Marcus asked at one point.

Cameron scoffed, 'If that's your concern, you should probably leave now.'

'I'm not going anywhere. I wasn't saying I was *worried* – it was just a question, that's all.'

'Well, it was a dumb one.'

The more I heard him speak, the less I liked Cameron. I got the impression he didn't know the others well but I suspected that his dickish behaviour would have continued even if they'd been his best friends.

He was just berating Marcus for his inability to sit still when a collective gasp erupted from the group. I wanted to move to see what had elicited such a dramatic response, but something told me to stay put.

'So, you are the ones saying goodbye to your old lives?'

Excitement coursed through me. I'd got it right: this was the group I was looking for. Only, it didn't sound like a kidnapping because Cameron, Marcus and the woman had *chosen* to come here.

When I crouched down and pulled Wilbur close, I was

surprised to feel the guttural resonance of a growl building in his belly. In all the years I'd known him, I'd barely heard him bark, let alone growl. Now was not the time for him to go full alpha. I needed him to stay quiet.

'Shhh, it's okay, boy. I've got you,' I whispered so quietly I could barely hear the words myself.

Wilbur's growl softened.

'Great Guardian,' the woman in the group said. 'You honour us with your presence.' Silence followed.

'Linda?' The one they'd called the Guardian spoke again. It was another female voice.

'Yes, Guardian?'

'You can stop the arse licking. You've signed your contract. Unless you feel like we'd break our word.'

'No, no!' Linda said hurriedly. 'I just read that it was good manners to show deference to your superiors, that's all.'

'You are correct in that regard, but I'm not one of those who merit your deference. In a few minutes you and I will be equals. Or close enough.' The Guardian's voice was unnaturally lyrical; it had a resonance, an almost ethereal quality that raised the hairs on the back of my arms. Maybe ethereal was the wrong word; maybe deadly would have been more accurate.

That feeling was compounded by the realisation that I hadn't heard her approach. There hadn't been a single crunch on the leaves. It didn't feel right, but somehow it made it more exciting.

'You'll do it here,' Cameron said. 'That's what we were told, that you would do it here. Will it happen right now?'

'That is the standard procedure.' The Guardian's tone was as soft as a breeze through the leaves. 'You have already been told that there is no turning back. If you are here there is only one way out – and one way or another it will be without a pulse.'

My own pulse raced faster still. Even in the autumn chill, I felt pinpricks of sweat forming on the back of my neck. For the first time, I regretted not bringing somebody with me but there was nothing I could do about it now.

Instead, I gulped down the lump in my throat and blew out at a slow, steady pace. My lungs were only half empty when the Guardian spoke again.

'There is someone else here.' The voice was sharp, accusing, and this time, I was the one who gasped. 'If any of you dared to tell—'

'It wasn't me!' Cameron said quickly. 'It must have been one of these two.'

'No, I didn't!'

'I would never!'

'Maybe it's just a dog walker,' Linda offered.

I was frozen to the spot, my back pressed against a tree. Maybe there were other people in the forest, and it wasn't me the Guardian had noticed. That wasn't impossible – after all, there had to be people who knew the forest well enough to walk through it at night. That was what I *hoped*, anyway.

Besides, that was the other reason I'd brought Wilbur with me: plausible deniability. I was just a dog walker seeking some solitude in a creepy wood. Perfectly normal, right?

'Well, what I said applies,' the Guardian continued. 'Nobody leaves here with a pulse.'

She was going to kill them; she'd just said so. But I didn't understand why these people sounded *excited* by the prospect. What wasn't I getting about this scenario? Was it a life-insurance scam? Was she talking about *faking* their deaths?

'Now, which of you is going first?'

'Me!' Cameron spoke up immediately. 'I've been on the waiting list for the last four years – and you've had my money all that time earning interest. I reckon I should get an extra person free for that. Not that there's anyone I'd want to bring on this little adventure.'

The sigh that left the Guardian's lips suggested she was as tired of hearing him talk as I was. She was going to do whatever he wanted just to shut him up – but I couldn't let that happen. I didn't care that these three had come here voluntarily; if the Guardian was going to take their lives, that made her a serial killer. You couldn't have someone like that loose on the streets. It just couldn't happen.

'You stay close to me, boy,' I whispered to Wilbur. 'I won't let anything happen to you.' As the words left my lips, I reconsidered. 'Unless you think you'll be safer running, then that's okay too. I won't hold it against you.'

I took a tentative step around the edge of the tree trunk and inched forward until I got my first proper look at the group. Unlike me, they had come with torches so for the first time all evening I could actually see more than an arm's length in front of my face.

I focused my attention on the group. To say they were a mismatched lot was putting it politely. As I'd suspected, Cameron was dressed in brogues and a suit; he looked more like the type of wedding guest who spent more on their tie than their gift than someone who'd been walking through a forest.

Marcus was mid-forties as well, and was wearing a comic-book T-shirt and jeans. Mum's basement: that was the thought that sprang to my mind. Not that we have many basements in the UK, so Mum's spare room, then.

As for Linda, she looked ... ordinary. She was in her late forties or early fifties, wearing jeans, Converse and what I guessed was a SuperDry hoodie or maybe a cheaper knockoff. I couldn't see much of her face, but her shoulders were hunched and she had an air of weariness, like someone who had the weight of life pushing her down.

But it was the other woman, the Guardian, who held my attention. She was dressed entirely in black: skinny black jeans, a black vest top and black heels. Red-soled stilettos.

There was no denying they were seriously hot shoes, but I would have struggled to wear them for a full day at the office – and I was good in heels. How on earth had she walked through the forest and not snapped one of them, or her ankle for that matter? Maybe I would ask her after I'd stopped her from carrying out mass murder.

She was standing less than a foot away from Cameron as he busied himself removing his tie and unbuttoning his shirt collar.

I had to do something, but what? What could I do that wouldn't put me at risk when I had no idea what was going on?

As I was standing there debating how to act, the Guardian grabbed Cameron by the hair, yanked his head to the side, exposed the length of his neck, and bit down. Hard.

This was seriously not good.

CHAPTER FIVE

My hand slackened on Wilbur's lead as my brain struggled to compute what I was seeing. It honestly looked like this Guardian, who had swept in silently in her killer heels, had plunged her teeth into Cameron's neck. Not only that, he had wanted her to. Why the hell would anyone want that?

One explanation circled around in my head, but it couldn't be right because what I was thinking was pure fantasy and I dealt in facts. Which meant she couldn't possibly be a vampire.

I willed the contents of my stomach to remain where they were as a bout of nausea swept through me. If I didn't keep control, I'd end up murdered in a pool of my own vomit; while I could deal with that, there was no way I'd be able to deal with the guilt of bringing Wilbur along with me. I couldn't defend him if I was dead – but the only way I'd stay alive was by taking out the murderer in the group.

I gripped the bottle of fake-pepper spray tightly, which was fairly pointless. If my overactive imagination was spot on and I was dealing with one of the undead, the only difference my weapon would make was to add a splash of colour to her black ensemble.

Praying that an answer would reveal itself to me, I glanced down at Wilbur. His eyes were on the group in front of us, but it was what was in his mouth that held my attention. Another broken branch, one with a very pointed end. More like a stake than a stick.

An insane thought took hold.

I had grown up on *Buffy*; I'd watched the DVD box set so many times I could tell you the episodes that had *all* the big plot twists – Tara's death, Spike's declaration, and the best musical episode of any series ever.

More than once, teenage me had dreamed about what it would be like to be called up as the slayer. Even so, I'd never thought it would happen.

I watched the scene unfolding. Linda and Marcus were staring with the same disbelief as I was as Cameron grew limper and limper in the Guardian's arms. I had to do something. *Now*.

Steeling myself for what was about to happen, I reached down, dropped the spray and grabbed the branch in Wilbur's mouth. He dropped it immediately into my palm, though from its sliminess we were still connected by a string or two of saliva.

I didn't waste time wiping my hand clean; instead I shifted my grip on the stick, dropped Wilbur's lead and charged.

There was no grace in the way I moved as my feet crashed through the undergrowth. It was only as I felt its weight that I realised just how long Wilbur's branch was. I must have looked like I was in some insane version of a jousting competition, only with no horse.

I was still six feet away when the Guardian released Cameron – or what remained of him. His body dropped to the ground and crunched the dry leaves. As she turned to face me, a slight smirk twisted the corner of her lips and she lazily lifted a hand to wipe a drop of blood from the side of her mouth.

Every instinct told me to run away, but instead I kept going straight towards her.

'I thought I heard someone,' she said. 'How nice of you to come out and play.' Her voice was laden with mockery. Lazy amusement curled her lips and revealed the blood-dipped fangs protruding from her gums. Yup, she was a freaking vampire.

That I was running straight at her in what I hoped was a threatening manner was clearly not an issue for her. She knew she had all the time in the world. Of course, she did. She could probably move at the speed of light or something ridiculous like that. I stood absolutely no chance.

Except—

That was when it hit me. I wasn't Buffy, who would stab a vampire through the heart right at the last second when their fangs were only inches from her neck. And much as I wished I looked hot in red-leather pants, I was more of a jogging bottoms' woman. I was me: Elodie Evergreen, investigative journalist with very, very limited sports' expertise. But by some miracle I realised that might actually be the thing to save me.

The stick I was holding was like a javelin: a little shorter, a bit thicker, but the physics were the same. And I could hit any target I wanted when I was throwing a javelin. Target practice for control had been one of my coach's warm-up drills, four times a week, every week for years. It wasn't about the strength you threw with, it was about reading the wind, maintaining your posture and knowing where you were aiming.

At that moment I knew exactly where I was aiming: at the breastbone of the bitch vampire who was still sneering at me.

I felt like I was back on the athletics field again – if the athletics field had been covered in trees. It was the dead of night when I could barely see my target and my aim was murdering someone rather than winning a competition, but hey, what did that matter? Linda's torch was still locked on the Guardian and that was the only thing I needed to see.

The branch hurtled through the air and I watched the vampire's sneer falter slightly, as if she were surprised. A millisecond later and the slightest crinkle formed between her brows. She lifted one of those six-inch stilettos by a fraction of an inch as she contemplated moving, but she'd spent too long watching what was about to happen rather than responding to it.

That same expression was still firmly in place when I heard the crunch of her breastbone.

A collective gasp shot through the forest – mine and

everyone else's, I think, but I didn't turn my head to check. My attention was still on the Guardian who had moved one of her hands to wrap it around the branch. If she pulled it out I was screwed, seriously screwed.

Yet before she had even straightened her elbow, her body disintegrated into a statue of dust. A heartbeat later, a slight gust of wind blew it away. Turns out Buffy wasn't as much of a fiction as I'd thought.

With my knees feeling like they'd been replaced with bubble tea I took a tentative step forward, only for Wilbur to rush straight past me to where the Guardian had been standing and dig his nose in the dirt.

'I'll find you another stick, boy,' I said. The very act of speaking made me nauseous. I had just staked a woman – no, I reminded myself, I had staked a *vampire*. She must have been because normal people didn't just turn into dust, did they? Surely there wasn't some genetic condition where bodies had so little hydration that they simply floated away after death?

'Wilbur,' I said, this time more firmly. His strangled bark seemed to ask me for a little more patience, but even so he lifted his head and I realised what he was doing: he hadn't been trying to pick up one item from the dirt at all, but two. Two impressively high stilettos with *red soles*. Stilettos that he brought straight over to me.

'That is a *very* good boy,' I said as he dropped them in front of me. They were slobbery but unscratched. It appeared that the luxury gifts for my valiant behaviour were already being delivered.

Now that the threat was gone, my pulse slowed a fraction and I turned to look at the two people who were still on their feet. Marcus had just emptied his stomach onto the forest floor, which I guessed would help feed the worms. It also confirmed him in my mind as a mummy's boy who'd never ventured out of the family home.

But it was Linda I couldn't draw my eyes away from, Linda who was looking at me with a face like thunder.

'What the hell have you just done?' she snarled.

CHAPTER SIX

The quietness in the forest shifted. Wilbur was back to digging in the dirt, possibly searching for more accessories that had survived the Guardian's flameless combustion, while Marcus was continuing to dry retch with such exaggeration I was sure he'd never been sick before. Above all that was the heavy thudding of my heart, an angry, confused thump caused by Linda's outburst.

'Sorry?' I said. Surely I must have misheard her – and yet she was continuing to look at me with the repulsion I'd have expected to get from a parent after I'd told them they had an ugly baby. Not that I'd done that, ever.

Assuming shock was the reason for her reaction, I pointed to Cameron's pale, dead body sprawled only three feet away from her. 'I'm pretty sure I just saved your life.'

'You idiot.' She shook her head then started pacing up and down. 'Do you have any idea how much money you've just cost me? Cost *us*!'

'I need a clean T-shirt,' Marcus said, wiping the vomit

from the mouth with the back of his hand. 'Did anyone pack any clean clothes I can borrow?'

'Oh, shut up,' Linda snapped. My initial impression that she was someone self-effacing who let others do the talking wasn't a hundred percent on the mark. 'We've got bigger things to deal with.'

Marcus wrinkled his nose as he finally caught onto what she was saying, even if I didn't have a clue. 'They'll still accept us, won't they?' he whined. 'This wasn't our fault. It was hers.'

'They'd better,' Linda replied. 'Otherwise, we're going to have some serious issues.' She glowered at me.

Although her teeth were reassuringly blunt compared to the Guardian's, I couldn't help thinking about the bottle of spray I'd dropped. Maybe I'd need it after all.

I took a step backwards, hoping to get closer to it. I had to distract her so she didn't notice I was up to something. 'We need to get him to a hospital.' I nodded towards Cameron.

I hadn't checked, but I seriously doubted he was still alive. But even if he was dead, his body didn't appear to be going pouf in the same way The Guardian's had, so he had to be dealt with through the proper channels. Police, forensics, that type of things.

'You're joking, right?' Linda replied. 'He's the only one who actually got what he paid for. I *knew* I should have insisted on going first but I just wanted the bloody man to shut up. Story of my life. I always think I'm doing something to keep the peace and who does it end up screwing? Me, that's who!'

'I'm sorry,' I said, shaking my head. 'I don't understand.'

I'd spotted the spray can only a few feet away. With a barely audible whistle, I called Wilbur over to my side. I didn't know what would happen next, but I wanted him next to me so I could tell him to run if he needed to.

As he raced over to me Linda gave a long sigh, the sort that a parent gives when they'd said the same thing forty times in twenty minutes yet their child is still none the wiser about what is being asked of them. Or the sigh of a boss who, despite having explained a task countless times, knows they'll end up doing the job themselves.

'They were going to turn us.' She rolled her eyes. 'You know, eternal youth? The eternal undead?'

'What?' I crouched down as if to stroke Wilbur and picked up the can. 'You mean you were going to become vampires?'

'Yes! And thanks to you, we have no idea what we're supposed to do now.'

'They were going to turn us and take us.' Marcus finally joined the conversation. He was now using a bunch of dried leaves to wipe down his T-shirt.

'Take you where?' I asked.

We were in a forest in the middle of nowhere. It was a long time since I'd done stranger-danger safety awareness at school, but I was pretty certain that meeting someone in a dark, secluded place – particularly someone with fangs –wouldn't end well. Wondering how the hell they could have thought otherwise I stood up, palming the can while maintaining eye contact with Marcus.

'We were going to join a community. A place we'd be accepted,' he said.

'A place where we wouldn't have to deal with all the bullshit of lame bosses, ungrateful husbands and bitter neighbours,' Linda added.

'But you get that they were just luring you here to kill you, right?' I was still gobsmacked they were acting so indignantly. It was one thing not to see that you were walking into a trap, but to stand in the middle of one when the door had already swung shut and think you were going to have a perfectly pleasant night suggested an extreme lack of brain cells.

Another emotion I didn't want to acknowledge mingled with my disbelief. Yes, they'd been tricked, but they had chosen to leave their entire lives behind. Leave their neighbours. Their jobs. Their families. The situation struck a little too close to home.

Quashing feelings of my mother, I went on, 'It was a trap to feed off you, like they fed off Cameron. Like they killed—' My words got stuck somewhere in my throat as I looked down at the ground, at the body that had fallen limply to the forest floor only minutes earlier.

Cameron was clambering to his feet, stretching his arms and clicking the cricks out of his neck. 'Well, that was one hell of a ride,' he said. 'I've got to tell you, those white lights are seriously bright.'

I edged back and pulled Wilbur tight to my side. Maybe I'd inhaled some mushroom spores as I'd walked through the forest. Maybe the Guardian hadn't actually appeared and I was on some hallucinogenic trip, curled up in bed while Andy reorganised the dishwasher for the third time before he joined me. There was a chance of that, no?

'It's okay, boy,' I whispered to Wilbur. 'I'll get you out of here, I promise.'

As the dog pushed against my legs, Cameron continued. 'What happened? Where is the Guardian? And why are you still human? My God you smell good!' He drew his tongue along his lips in a way that made me want to empty my stomach, yet Linda didn't look the slightest bit phased.

'I wouldn't risk biting us. Remember the rules. You do that and they'll kill you. Speaking, of which...' Linda turned to me. 'We have a problem. *She* killed the Guardian. She's stopped us from getting what we paid for.'

Cameron sneered. 'That sounds like *your* problem,' he scoffed. 'And that's why you always insist on going first.'

If it wouldn't have pushed me into the realms of serial vampire killer, I probably would have done the javelin trick a second time. But I'd seen this guy as a human and it didn't feel right; besides, he wasn't actually doing anything other than being a dick.

With an arrogant chuckle, he started to move away. Linda stepped in front of him. 'You need to turn us,' she said.

'What?' He gave a laugh but it caught in his throat. 'No, I don't.'

'Yes, you do,' Linda said. 'Because if you don't, I'll tell them that you were the one who killed the Guardian.'

'You wouldn't!'

'Yes, I would. And you know what they said they'd do to anyone who disobeys their orders. They'll hunt you down. You'll get a week – maybe even less.'

Cameron snarled.

Despite being scared shitless and struggling to see a way out of the situation that didn't involve more killing, I was impressed by Linda. She kept her head under pressure, or at least she could act that way to get what she wanted. I suspected she'd been pushed into this situation by idiots like Cameron. This felt like her last resort, and when people reach the stage in life where they have nothing more to lose they can be even more dangerous than the fools with the fangs.

'They won't buy it,' Cameron said finally

'Yes, they will,' Linda replied. 'It'll be two against one. Three, if we include her.'

I didn't want to be included. What I wanted was to take Wilbur home and have a very stiff drink. I had the feeling that wasn't going to happen.

Still gripping Wilbur's lead and the paint can, I watched as Cameron considered Linda's offer. 'Even if I agreed, I don't know how to turn you,' he said.

'Who didn't do their research properly?' Linda smirked. 'From everything I read, it's very simple. You just have to make sure you pump venom out through your fangs when you bite us. If we don't die from losing too much blood then you'll need to snap our necks.'

'And what if I get it wrong?' Cameron said. 'What if I drain your blood and kill you without getting enough venom into your system? Then what? I'll have just killed you. Is that a risk you want to take?'

Linda bit down on her bottom lip.

'You're right. It's not,' she said thoughtfully – and then she smiled. Unpleasantly. 'Which is why you're going to practise on her first.'

Oh hell. No, he wasn't.

CHAPTER SEVEN

Wilbur gave a faint whine and I wanted to do the same. We were up shit creek without a paddle. Any relief I'd felt when the Guardian turned to dust evaporated as I frantically looked around for another improvised stake.

'I agree,' Marcus said before I could object. 'Test it on her, then do it to us when you know it works. It only took a few minutes for you to come back round. That's fine.'

I was starting to think I preferred Marcus when he was throwing up his guts and couldn't speak.

'So we're agreed?' Linda asked.

'I guess.' Cameron shrugged.

'Good. Let's get started. And you probably want to drain her to kill her. The blood lust is supposed to be terrible after you've first been turned, so you probably won't be able to stop. Plus it'll give you more time to get the venom into her.'

'I'm sorry,' I said, unable to stay silent any longer. 'You can't be serious. You're just—? You're just gonna kill me?'

Linda looked aghast. 'Of course not! You'll get the greatest gift – immortality. And for free. I had to clean out my pension to afford this. Obviously if it doesn't work, then yes, you'll be dead – but that's absolutely not our intention.'

She was insane. One hundred percent fruit loop. That had to be the only explanation. She couldn't possibly think this was acceptable behaviour.

'I don't want this,' I said firmly 'I'm human, and perfectly happy as a human. I have a job that I love. I have a boyfriend – fiancé! I am not okay with you murdering me!'

Cameron joined in the debate. 'You're just being shortsighted. Trust me, if you knew what we knew, all the incredible gifts you'd get.' He closed his eyes and drew in a long breath like a superhero in a movie getting ready for their big battle. 'I can feel it in my veins, the nuances of sense. The power, the strength—'

'The fact you'll vaporise the second sunrise hits you?' I countered. Given that turning to dust from a stake through the heart had been true, I assumed the sunlight thing was too.

Linda waved a hand dismissively. 'There are ways around that – wards, potions, all sorts of things. We're offering you a gift, a once-in-a-lifetime chance.' She smiled tightly. 'Although let's be honest, we're not really *offering*. You brought this on yourself. Actions have consequences, including yours.'

She looked at Cameron. 'Do you need us to hold her down? Or do you think you can do this yourself?'

'Oh, I think I can do it,' he said with an overconfident smirk.

Strange as it was, in that moment one of the thoughts rolling through my head was how much I wished it wasn't him. Of all the people who could have killed me, why did it have to be some middle-aged, arrogant man who thought he was God's gift? How was that fair?

I didn't want him to be the one to drain my blood, to put his venom in me – the thought made me gag. Still, whatever fate awaited me, Wilbur didn't deserve to be part of it. I reached down and unclipped his lead. 'Run!' I said as he looked up at me. 'You need to run to the car, okay? Run and find people.'

He didn't move, but instead let out a low whine. Wilbur wasn't the type of dog to leave someone's side, not when he was loyal to them, which meant I had to make him go.

Channelling my fear and praying he misread it as anger, I raised my voice to a shout. 'Go, Wilbur! Leave me! Now!' He whined again but this time he listened and backed up several feet. 'Go!' I shouted again. I hated this, but I was trying to save him.

He ran, slowly at first then faster. I heard his feet crunch on the leaves then fade into nothing.

My muscles turned limp as I propped myself up against the nearest tree. When I lifted my head, Cameron was only a foot away from me. Damn his vampire speed and stealth.

'You know, a lot of women would consider themselves lucky to get this close and personal with me,' he said. His lips twitched and he waggled his eyebrows in what I suspected he thought was a sexy fashion. It actually looked as if someone had applied an electric current directly to his forehead.

'If that's the case, it's only because this is how close they'd have to be to do this,' I replied.

Before he realised what was about to happen, I'd raised my knee and driven it straight between his legs. 'I'm assuming the nuances of "sense" also cover that part of the male anatomy?' I scoffed as he doubled over. 'Though I've always heard that it's particularly sensitive.'

He growled, ready to lunge at me, but the instant his head lifted I slammed my finger down on the trigger of the can with all my force. Red paint splattered into his face; from the way he hissed, it obviously packed a punch.

He staggered back, clawing at his eyes. 'Stop her!' he yelled to the others. 'Don't let her get away!'

Marcus and Linda jumped into action but I was ready with my spray. Keeping my finger firmly on the trigger I turned my arm in an arc, indiscriminately shooting red paint at everything in front of me. The fumes were pungent, and one deep breath was all it took for my eyes to start watering, but I could cope with a bit of discomfort if it meant I got out of there alive.

Apparently the same couldn't be said for Marcus. The minute he saw he was about to get a face full, he cowered and jump backwards. Linda didn't flinch, however; that woman was tough as nails. The top of her head had received a patchy dye job courtesy of yours truly, and some paint had dribbled down towards her eyes, but I'd need a much better shot to stop her completely. For that to happen I had to get closer.

When she lunged to grab my wrist, I let her. Only when she thought she'd got a decent hold did I pull her sharply towards me. Her balance faltered and I was there, ready. The can lined was up with her eyes as I pressed again.

Nothing.

Shit

I tried again. As I grappled to hold her in place, the can offered a watery hiss and a weak dribble of paint.

I looked around, hoping for another way out, only to see Marcus on one side of me and Cameron on the other.

'You can't escape,' Linda said. 'You should stop struggling. You'll only make it more painful.'

'Fu—'

No doubt Linda knew exactly what I was about to say, but before I could finish the word Cameron had grabbed hold of me, twisted my arm around my back – and plunged his teeth into my neck.

My body stiffened as pain shot through me, sharp and deep, but the force of my panic was worse. Though my instincts screamed at me to fight, his grip was ironclad. Why, oh why, had I leaned *into* Linda? Why hadn't I just *run*?

There was nothing I could do. Cameron was holding me tightly, and panic and pain were freezing my brain and my limbs. A sickening wave of dizziness hit me as I felt my blood being pulled from my body.

At least Wilbur had got away, I thought, as I grew more and more light-headed. At least Wilbur had got away...

And there, somewhere in the chaos, another ridiculous thought rose to the surface: I wished I'd had a dog of my own, my own Wilbur. I wished I'd convinced Andy that we should get a dog. If I survived this, that would be at the top of my bucket list.

Not that I would survive it. I could feel it already: I was dying, a pet-less journalist in the middle of a forest. Maybe I'd get a dog in my next life, I thought. Yes, a dog in my next life would have to do.

As I was considering what breed I'd choose as my loyal companion, something shifted. My thoughts were growing more lucid. I could smell a dog, feel fur against my skin. And the pain? The pain was gone. The sensation of teeth in my neck had disappeared; instead, there was a strange wetness against my hand.

As I blinked open my eyes and saw brown eyes looking back at me, my heart leapt – and then sank. Wilbur had come back for me.

I was opening my mouth, ready to tell him to go again, when a scream shot into the night.

'No! No, it can't be!' Suddenly aware that I was no longer being held, I turned around to find Linda on her knees, her head buried in her hands.

CHAPTER EIGHT

Usually, I wasn't a person who was easily confused. Testament to that was that I actually knew where the various congestion-charge zones were in London and, trust me, that was no mean feat. But goddamn it, I had no idea what was going on.

If anyone should have been on the floor crying, surely it was me? I was the one who'd just had my body drained by a vampire. Only I was standing up with Wilbur at my side, which surely meant I was still alive. But then Cameron had also stood up after he'd been killed by a vampire, so what did it mean? Was I dead? Undead? And if that was the case, why the hell was Linda bawling? Had she suddenly found a conscience? That didn't seem likely. And Marcus? Well, he appeared to be comforting her.

'Okay, boy,' I whispered to Wilbur. 'I think this is our cue to get out of here. Properly this time.'

His lead was still on the ground. I was in two minds

whether to put it on him, but I didn't want him running off so I didn't have much choice.

I'd barely opened the clasp when Linda was back on her feet, pointing her finger at me. 'You knew this would happen, didn't you?' Her voice was trembling, though whether it was from fear, anger or a mixture of both I couldn't tell. 'You *wanted* him to turn you so this would happen.'

'I'm sorry, you've lost me,' I said.

'Cameron! He's dead. He ... he poufed!' She raised her hands in case I didn't know what she meant by 'poufed.'

Sure enough, there was no sign of Cameron, though even in semi-darkness I could pick out the larger than average quantity of grey dust amid the leaf litter. Grey dust exactly where Cameron had been standing.

'How?' I asked, utterly confused.

'How?' Linda looked like I'd just slapped her across the face. 'He poufed when he was turning you,' she spat. 'I don't know how you did it, but this is on you. You planned it, didn't you? That's why you're here, because someone sent you. Someone sent you to kill the Guardian and everyone like them. What are you, some kind of vampire hunter?'

I turned around in a circle hoping that someone was going to jump out from behind a tree and tell me I'd been spunked or punked or whatever you called it, but there was no one. No one except Marcus, who was scratching his head with such ferocity that I wanted to offer him Wilbur's flea collar.

'Are you freaking kidding me?' I said. I couldn't listen

to another word of her drivel. No wonder she had problems with her neighbours; ten minutes into knowing this woman and I wanted to erect a very large fence between us.

'No, I'm not a bloody vampire hunter, I'm a journalist. I'm Elodie Evergreen and I'm here following a lead. A missing persons' lead. Why the hell would I want this? You ... you tried to kill me!'

'Tried? How sweet.' she scoffed.

It only took me a second to realise what she meant: Cameron had killed me. That strange dizziness, that moment when my clouded thoughts suddenly became clear again. That had been the transition.

'What do we do?' Marcus asked. He was no longer paying any attention to me but looking at Linda. 'Is there someone we could call? I can't go back to my mum's. She's really mad at me – I may have stolen money from her cruise fund to pay for this.'

Linda pouted. 'Maybe we could find our way to one of the communities. Tell them what happened.'

'Will they let us in? We're not magical.'

'But that's not our fault, is it? It's *hers*.'

She jabbed her finger at me and I was struck with an almost overwhelming urge to grab it and yank it clean out of its socket. I'd heard that several cultures considered it rude to point, and I was starting to understand why.

Still, I could feel the energy surging through my body; if I took hold of her finger, I'd probably pull off her entire arm. That meant that for the first time since I had walked into the forest I most definitely had the upper hand.

'Look,' I said, decisively. 'Whatever you two have got yourselves into – all this talk of magical communities – I'm having nothing to do with it. You're on your own.'

When I moved to leave, I was surprised by how quickly my body responded and how quiet my footsteps were. Everything around me looked so clear; the moon was still shrouded by clouds, and yet I could make out the colours in the fallen leaves and the textures in the gnarled bark of the trees. I could hear the slightest of rustling, from the mouse that was scurrying through the undergrowth by our feet, to the barn owl preening its feathers a little way to my left.

With a prickling sensation that raised the hairs on the back of my neck, I turned and tilted my gaze upwards. Sure enough, exactly where I'd thought, a barn owl was perched on a branch, its gaze locked on me.

Shit. This was insane. I was trying not to think about the fact that I was technically dead – but I was also starting to understand why these people had emptied their bank accounts to do this.

'It's not going to work,' Linda said softly. 'You can't go back to your old life. They won't let you be. We'll tell them what you did, how you killed two of their own, and they'll hunt you down.'

In one short stride, I was inches from her face. Every detail of her complexion, from the thin red veins in her eyes to the slight indents on the sides of her nose, was crystal clear.

'I have a life. A fiancé,' I said. 'I don't care what happens to you. You can stay in this forest for the rest of your lives for all I care, but I'm leaving. And you don't have a single way of stopping me.'

Her eyes flickered to the ground to the stake I had used on the Guardian. I laughed. 'Really?' I said. 'That won't work. Trust me.'

Before she could blink, it was in my hand. Now I understood what Cameron had been talking about – the sensitivity, the strength – though he'd neglected to mention the queasiness. Maybe he'd just taken a lot of antacids in preparation. Vampires and antacids: those weren't two words I'd ever hear in the same sentence.

'Now, I need a minute to think about the best way to handle this.' I looked at Marcus and then at Linda. 'Then we can talk.'

I was cursing myself for having given them my real name. How bloody stupid was that? At the very least, I should have given a fake one, something to stop them from tracing me. And now, much as I wanted to, I couldn't leave. These two might only be humans, but they were humans who knew how to contact vampires.

I didn't want to admit it, but my rapid reflexes and heightened senses suggested that I was also a vampire. A vampire who had killed the only other one of my type that I'd met.

'You're not turning me,' Linda muttered. 'There's something wrong with you. The way Cameron died – who knows how much you'd mess it up.'

I gritted my teeth. Maybe it would be kinder to change her if only to remove her from the rest of humanity.

As I was mulling over my options, my phone rang in

my pocket. Donna. I'd missed three calls from her and two messages that had come through while I was dealing with the Guardian and Cameron.

I moved my thumb to hang up – and then I stopped. I could trust Donna with anything, couldn't I? She was my best friend, not to mention an incredible journalist. She had broken stories that had people threatening her if she refused to reveal her sources, threatening her career, her life, her everything, and she had never disclosed a single one. She was strong and smart and everything I needed right now.

Other than the row we'd had about my story, she'd always had my back – and it was hard to deny that she'd been right about me not coming here. If there was anyone I could talk to, it was her – assuming she didn't think I'd lost the plot. That was a very real possibility; I was well aware how completely nuts it sounded, but what choice did I have? I needed an ally – and one was ringing me.

My scalp prickled. It was like the fates were intervening. Suddenly aware of the eerie silence in my chest – no heartbeat – I answered the call.

'Elodie, thank God! Tell me you didn't go to Sydenham Hill Wood? Please.'

I could hear the fear in Donna's voice, the way her vocal chords tightened as the air passed by them. But why would she sound afraid? Unless she already knew there was something to be scared of.

'Yes, about that...' I cleared my throat. 'I might need a little help.'

CHAPTER NINE

Donna pinged me a location, a car park about a mile from where we were. Although she'd said she was happy to walk into forest to find me, I managed to persuade her not to. The last thing I needed was for something to happen to her, too. It was bad enough that I'd brought Wilbur into this mess, although he seemed perfectly content carrying one red-soled shoe in his mouth while the other was stuffed deep in my pocket.

Part of me wanted to see if he'd swap it for a stick; I didn't think shoes like these coped well with slobber, but I could buy more shoes and after what we'd been through, I owed him.

So instead, we were walking to Donna. About ten minutes after we started our trek, Linda and Marcus tried to make a run for it. Thanks to their less-than-subtle whispering and my new miraculous hearing, I was well aware of their plans before they were afoot.

'I'll go in a different direction,' Marcus whispered. 'She can't follow us both.'

'Fine,' Linda agreed. 'On my countdown. Three, two, one...'

It was the first time I'd had a chance to test my speed – and it was *fun*. Seriously fun. I gave them a few seconds so I could see if I was as fast as I suspected, but it turned out I was even faster. My legs whipped through the air and my hair billowed behind me as the cold night breeze rushed against my skin. Even Wilbur couldn't keep up.

I grabbed Marcus by the shoulder, hoisted him six inches off the ground and dragged him over to where Linda was wheezing after running less than ten meters. How the hell she'd thought she could get away from *anyone* was a mystery, let alone a supernatural assailant.

I slammed Marcus down next to her then stood in front of them. 'I might not know as much about what I am as you guys do,' I said, 'but I'm a fast learner. I won't have any problem running like this for hours. You, on the other hand...'

'You don't deserve that speed. Those gifts. You didn't pay for them,' Linda snarled.

'Oh, I can assure you I did,' I said dryly. With my life.

In what was clearly a moment of insanity, she lunged at me. Maybe she hoped I'd bite down on her and she'd get her wish, but a single step to the side was all I needed to take me out of her reach.

And that was when I felt it. A wave of weakness rolled through my body, like the life was once again being drained from it.

I gasped and my head snapped up just in time to see a gap in the shadows as moonlight filtered through. A second later, the clouds shifted, covered the moon once more and the feeling faded. Moonlight? Did vampires have a problem with moonlight?

I was no longer in any doubt as to what I was. Several times during the walk, I'd tried to find my pulse but there was nothing, not a hint. But if I *was* a vampire, why had Cameron died when he turned me? Was that normal? It hadn't happened to the Guardian, though maybe that was because I'd got there in time to drive my stake through their chest.

Maybe that was the reason these vampires were being turned, some kind of one in, one out rule. But that would be insane. Why would the Guardian agree to turn anyone unless she was carrying out some sort of bizarre ritual suicide?

With every moment that passed, my list of questions was getting longer. The problem was, I didn't know who to ask.

'Elodie?' Despite telling Donna to wait for me *outside* the forest, she appeared through the dense foliage.

'Don't come too close to me,' I said quickly. 'I'm not sure ... I'm not sure that I'm *safe*. Can you call Wilbur?'

'Wilbur? As in Sonia's dog, Wilbur?'

'I may have brought him with me. Go on, boy. Go to Donna.'

With the shoe still in his mouth, Wilbur raced over to Donna and dropped it at her feet.

'And what about us?' Linda snapped from behind me. 'Are we just meant to stand here?'

'Yes,' I replied. 'Stand there and be quiet until I know what we're going to do.'

Although I worried that I was now a vampire and my very existence could put Donna in danger, I reasoned that if I'd wanted to kill someone by now it would have been Linda. Linda and then Marcus. Given that they were still alive, I obviously wasn't an immediate danger to anyone around me. They were both incredibly annoying, but they were still breathing: I definitely had some self-control.

Still, I needed to talk to Donna openly and I couldn't do that with them listening over my shoulder. 'You two, stay here.' I offered them my most vicious glare, which I was pretty sure only looked as if I were squinting or had something in my eye. I might have to work on that. 'You make any attempt to run and I will come for you. Do you understand?'

Marcus nodded, and the sound of him gulping was all the confirmation I needed that he'd do exactly what I'd said. Linda, on the other hand, scowled.

With a strange sense of nervousness, I walked towards Donna. She was now holding the shoe that Wilbur had given her. I was almost overwhelmed with the urge to hug her, and for a split second my arms were wide, ready to do just that, but I stopped and pulled back.

'Donna, something happened in the forest,' I said quietly. 'Someone did something to me. They changed me.'

'No! Shit!' She dropped her head and groaned. 'Elodie!

Why, oh why did you come here when I specifically told you not to? I should have known you wouldn't drop it.'

I'd opened my mouth to continue my explanation when it struck me: Donna hadn't asked what had happened or how I'd 'changed'. The cogs in my brain whirred and arrived at the only possible explanation.

'You know, don't you?' I was aware of the tremble in my voice. 'That's why you didn't want me to come here, wasn't it? Not because there isn't a story but because you already knew what was happening.'

Donna let out a controlled breath, so slow I felt I could hear every individual molecule of oxygen moving from her lungs into the air. 'It's complicated,' she said finally. 'Very complicated.'

My hand flew to my mouth. 'Oh my God. Are you – are you one, too? Are you a – a *vampire*?'

She shook her head. 'I'm not...' She hesitated then glanced toward Linda and Marcus. 'This isn't the place to talk about it. Have they been turned too?'

'No. Things got a little *complicated*,' I said, throwing the word back in her face.

I felt more winded now than I had when I'd been drained of blood. Donna had known about the existence of vampires and she hadn't told me. Clearly she trusted me less than I trusted her, and that stung more than a little.

'Right. Well, let's get them sorted, then get back to the office. We can talk there.'

I was torn. Donna was my boss and my best friend, but by not telling me the truth she had put me in danger.

She was responsible for what I had become – and she'd didn't seem particularly alarmed. Why the hell wasn't she terrified of me? *I* was terrified of me.

I wanted answers and she didn't have the strength to force me to go anywhere. I folded my arms across my chest to make it perfectly clear I was staying put.

'You know we'll freeze if we have to stay out here all night,' Linda moaned. 'Some of us still have a body temperature to maintain.'

Then again, I also wanted Linda out of my hair as soon as possible. 'Fine,' I said to Donna as I unfolded my arms. 'I'll come with you. But you have some serious explaining to do.'

With a nod she moved past me and addressed Linda and Marcus. 'I take it you paid for a service that was supposed to happen here tonight? Let me guess – you dealt with a third party? It was all hush-hush and someone with some secret code name bullshit like The Saviour was meant to meet you?'

'It was The Guardian,' Marcus answered.

Linda cut across him. 'Yes, we've paid. And don't try any bullshit about offering us a refund. We want what we were promised – and compensation, too. She's the one who screwed it up. She killed the Guardian – *and* our friend.'

Donna glanced at me. 'Really?'

'He was hardly their friend,' I objected. 'She'd only known him a couple of hours and she hated his guts. And I didn't *kill* him – he died when he turned me.'

An expression I couldn't decipher flashed across

Donna's face before she turned back to Linda and Marcus. 'My car's parked at the edge of the forest. Let's go.'

'Where are you taking us?' Linda whinged.

'I just told you, to my car. When we get there, you two will get in the back and wait. I need to speak to Elodie alone for a moment then we'll deal with getting you what you paid for.'

Donna's voice was incredibly calm, although anyone who was familiar with her knew that was the time you needed to fear her most. Yup, if my suspicions were right, things weren't going to improve for Linda and Marcus tonight.

CHAPTER TEN

Donna unlocked the car and opened the back door for Linda and Marcus before turning to Wilbur and me. 'Wilbur, you stay here with Elodie, okay?' As she moved to the driver's seat, she lowered her voice to a whisper. 'I'll be one minute, Elodie. Put your fingers in your ears and count to thirty.'

'Sorry?' I muttered only to realise my mistake. She'd obviously lowered her voice deliberately, once again confirming she knew that my new state came with some enhancements. Still, I took a moment before I obeyed; instead I watched her opening the driver's door while simultaneously pulling something from her pocket before sliding inside and shutting the door behind her.

I was tempted to leave my ears unblocked. It wasn't that I didn't trust Donna, but the journalist part of me knows that it's the things that are said behind closed doors that you really want to hear. Still, I needed to trust her –and she'd said I couldn't listen, not that I couldn't watch.

Annoyingly, the angle I was at made it difficult to see what was going inside the car without crouching. All I could make out was a small glow that came from inside the vehicle as if Donna had just switched on the internal light. Before I saw anything else, I was struck by the same feeling of weakness – and this time it was strong enough to make me drop to my hands and knees.

'Crap,' I gasped, finally channelling enough strength to look up. Once again the full moon was shining down on us, but this time the clouds didn't seem in any hurry to close over it.

I was still on the ground, fangs out and gravel digging into my palms, when Donna reappeared. She dashed to my side. 'Elodie, what's going on? Did you listen to the spell?'

'Spell?' I wheezed, taking a breath and then another. 'What spell?'

Her face crinkled with confusion. 'I just wiped their memories with a spell. Did you listen? Isn't that what did this? Vampires can respond strangely to some magic.'

I shook my head but even that small action sent a searing pain rolling through the base of my skull. 'The moon,' I said. 'I think it's... I think it's...'

I couldn't even get the words out; it was as if the strength was wicking from my body and returning to the earth. How the hell did I not know that the moon affected vampires? Why did none of the books write about this? Damn fiction!

I was clasping my head and squeezing my eyes shut when the feeling finally eased. Shifting my gaze upwards, I saw wispy clouds blocking out most of the moonlight. I had no doubt I'd soon have the same sensation again soon if I didn't get inside.

Shit, if this was how bad moonlight was, what the hell would sunlight do to me? Would I never feel its warmth on my face again?

'Come on.' Donna helped me up. 'Let's get you into the car, drop these two off, and then we can talk.'

In the back of the car, Linda and Marcus were chatting away merrily.

'Well, I've never done a car share before,' Marcus was saying. 'But yes, I can see that it's very good for the environment. Very good. Maybe I should have had a couple less drinks, though. Everything's a bit fuzzy at the minute.'

'I'm the same. Were we drinking cocktails?' Linda replied. 'It's a strange place for cocktails, isn't it? And oh, there's a dog! I love dogs. Well, most dogs. My neighbours got these chihuahuas, yappy little things. And there's this massive mastiff thing up the road – I don't like that, either. But they're better than cats. Don't get me started on cats.'

I glanced at Donna, who shot me a look warning me to stay quiet. Wilbur was in the footwell, resting his head on my lap. I still felt bad about putting him in danger; whatever happened with me and my future, he'd be getting gift boxes of treats for the rest of his doggy days.

'Right, here we are,' Donna said eventually.

'Sydenham Tube Station. It's been such a great night. Bye!'

Marcus opened the door and slid out of the car. Linda waited a moment longer. 'Do we do this regularly?' she asked. 'I can't seem to remember.'

'No, this was very much a one-off,' I answered.

'Oh, well, I'm sure it was fun.' A moment later, she stumbled out of the car.

'What did you do to them?' I asked Donna as they staggered towards the tube.

She shrugged. 'Nothing that they won't be grateful for in the long run. It was just a memory-loss spell, though it's quite a powerful one. It'll get rid of everything they saw tonight, any lingering thoughts they had about vampires or magical communities.'

'You're ... you're a witch?' I said.

Donna looked at me as if she was about to flash a smile, then her expression darkened. 'Elodie, if I'd had any idea that you were going there—'

'It's ... it's fine,' I said. 'It's not your fault. I'm the one who disobeyed an order.'

'Yes, you did,' she agreed. 'And it's the magical government's fault for not stamping on these damn pirates before now – they know how many people have gone missing. But it's my fault you were there. Part of my role is to be a bridge between our world and yours, to keep magic hidden, control the press so that information doesn't get out. You have to shoulder part of the blame for being so damned stubborn, but I shouldn't have let that happen.'

'You're a witch,' I repeated, even though she hadn't confirmed it. 'You've always been a witch.'

'I'm sorry I've had to lie to you.'

In terms of screwing with my head, the day was turning into a masterclass. My best friend was a witch, I was a vampire? What the hell? Was Wilbur secretly a werewolf?

I glanced down at my jeans and saw a large patch of drool spreading over the denim. No, I was pretty sure that wasn't the case – although if witches and vampires were real, there was probably a good chance werewolves were, too.

'So those people tonight had been targeted by pirates? What does that mean?'

'There's a lot we need to talk through,' Donna said.

Before she could say any more, my stomach growled so loudly that Wilbur yelped. I hadn't really thought about being hungry – I'd had a bit of a snack before I'd left home. There again, I'd walked a darn sight more than I did on an average evening.

Donna pointed to the glove box. 'In there,' she said, a strange note in her throat.

I opened it expecting to find a granola bar or a packet of crisps but instead I saw a clear plastic bag filled with a viscous red liquid. Stuck to the side of it was a thin yellow straw. It reminded me of the Capri Sun drinks my mum used to get me after my weekend swimming lessons – though I suspected the company would be inundated with complaints if they extended their beverage selection to include this.

For a moment all I could do was gawp. 'You're not serious?' I said finally.

'Just poke a straw in the top,' she said. 'I take it you didn't feed when you were turned?'

'No. It's all a bit of a daze. I didn't even see the vampire who turned me die. Apparently he just kind of ... poufed.' I replicated the gesture Linda had made with my hands. If I never said the word pouf again, it would be too soon.

'That's unusual.' Donna frowned. 'What about the other? The one who called herself the Guardian?'

'Well, you did mention me brushing up on my javelin skills.'

Her eyebrows rose. 'You staked her?'

'I did.' I glanced down at the blood. There was no way I could drink it; even if it wasn't from a human, it was gross. And no matter how much my stomach grumbled, there were things I needed more than blood. Like answers. Even though I was dead, the journalist side of me was very much alive.

'Donna, who was the Guardian? Why was she turning humans into vampires?'

She sighed. 'Why does anybody do anything?' she said. 'Money, that's why. There are always people willing to pay and people looking for a shortcut. Guardian?' She scoffed. 'The name makes me cringe. They aren't guardians of anything. They're letting people who have no business in the magical world access to it.' Another sigh billowed from her lips before she looked across at me.

'You have some decisions to make tonight, Elodie, and

they'll be a lot easier to make on a full stomach. So please, just drink that blood for me then we can talk. Properly.'

CHAPTER ELEVEN

I was doing an excellent job of looking like I was about to drink the blood. I took the straw off the side and turned it over in my hand several times. I picked up the bag and sniffed it deeply – though that had been a mistake. I'd expected to get nothing but the smell of plastic, but a hit of iron struck right at the back of my throat. My gums tingled in a way no person's gums were meant to tingle.

This wasn't just a blood bag; drinking blood meant I truly understood and accepted what I was becoming – what I had *become*. I put the bag down on my lap and looked at Donna. 'My life's changed, hasn't it? Forever?' I asked.

'Yes and no. Of course, the sunlight will make it difficult for you to continue working your usual hours but you're a journalist – you're one of *my* journalists. If you want to stay on at the paper, we can make it happen.'

'I want to stay on,' I said without a moment's hesitation. My work was my life and I hadn't even considered that I could lose my job. I hadn't spent nearly a decade working my way up for one night – and one bite – to ruin all my dreams. 'What about my friends? Andy? Am I safe around them?'

'You were safe around those two, weren't you?' she said pointedly. 'And I'm perfectly happy to be in a car with you.'

'You're a witch,' I retorted. 'Judging by the way you just addled their brains, you could get me to leave this car believing I was a pine cone if that was what you wanted.'

Donna chuckled. 'That might push my powers a little, but I know what you're saying. Every vampire is different, but as long as you don't let yourself get hungry no one should be in danger.'

I should have been relieved, but I wasn't. I was the type of person who became hangry; I was known for biting people's heads off if I was ten minutes late getting lunch. Figuratively speaking. Now it could literally happen.

'Realistically,' Donna said, sensing my nervousness – or rather my blind terror, 'you'll probably want to move into a magical community.'

'A magical community?' I raised my eyebrows; of all the things I'd seen and heard, I didn't know why that was the one that surprised me most.

'Assuming you want to stay in London, there are a couple of places. Camden obviously has one – half the people in Camden are paras. But Peckham is gaining popularity, too.'

'Paras?'

'Paranormals,' Donna replied, as though it were the most natural thing in the world 'Witches, werewolves, sirens—'

'Sirens? You're not serious.' I laughed. 'Next you'll be telling me that mermaids are real!' Her look said it all. 'There are *mermaids* in London?'

She wrinkled her nose. 'Not that I know of. For obvious reasons most of them live on the coast, and the biggest communities are outside the cities where they can shield themselves more easily. But I guess there might be some mermaids living in canals since they've cleaned them up in recent years. It's probably something I should look into.'

'This is ... weird.' I wished there was a word that more accurately described the complete upheaval my life had just gone through. Every variation of a future I had imagined for myself was bust now: sunset walks, over; days at the beach a no-go. Yes, my job was one of the most important parts of my life but it wasn't my *whole* life. I still needed other things, didn't I?

How the hell could I explain my sudden aversion to sun to Andy? Not to mention the drastic change in the contents of our fridge.

'It feels like there are things I should do,' I said, hoping a proactive approach would detract from the terror that was gradually consuming me. 'Do I need to register myself as a ... a para? Is there a vampire government I need to report to, or just a general magical one? And what do I do about the vampires I killed? Shit, am I going to go to para prison on my first day of being undead?'

Panic was rising through me – and panic without a pulse is a weird thing. There was still a drumming in my body as if my muscles, my lungs, my stomach were contracting, but no pounding heartbeat.

'I'll take care of everything I can.' Donna reached out and squeezed my arm gently. 'I can take you back to the office, answer your questions – as far as I can – or I can take you home. I'll stay with you when you speak to Andy, if you want, so you're not alone when he finds out. It might be easier for me to answer his questions. Assuming you want to tell him, that is?'

Her expression implied I had a choice, but did I? Andy was my fiancé so surely he *had* to know. We hadn't set a date and time for the wedding, but he'd find it strange if I suddenly wanted a late-night ceremony.

How the hell would he cope with me being a vampire? The idea of having a pet or pollen in the house was enough to have him scratching his skin!

But this was me, the love of his life, we were talking about. And it wasn't like I was going to start shedding fur. If I'd been changed into a werewolf that would have been a serious problem, but surely he couldn't have an issue with me being a vampire. As long as I didn't start drinking from him.

I tried to imagine what I would have done if our roles were reversed. As long as he was still my Andy – the way I was certain that I was still *me* – I couldn't see a problem. If he were the vampire, I would stand by him. Of course I would. I was sure he'd do the same.

I had decided: I was going to tell him. And it would be fine. 'Let's go to mine,' I said, feeling the tension shift in my body. 'Andy deserves to know.'

CHAPTER TWELVE

'For crying out loud, drink that bloody blood,' Donna said as we parked outside my flat. 'You don't want to go in there hungry. Emotions can go haywire after a change. It'll settle you, calm you down. Drink it. Now.'

That Donna thought imbibing any sort of bodily fluid could be calming showed how screwed up my situation was, but there was no way I wanted to put anyone at risk. My body count was already at two and I didn't want it to go up.

Scrunching my eyes closed, I stuck the straw into the plastic and took a gulp. 'Urgh, that's all I can manage,' I said as a thick mouthful oozed down my throat.

'No, it's not. Come on, you'll get used to it,' Donna insisted.

Aware that I was crinkling up my nose like a toddler being forced to eat their broccoli, I looked at the bag again. That mouthful hadn't even made a dent in it. 'Can't you put a spell on it? Make it taste like piña colada or something?'

She chuckled. 'I can't say I've ever tried it, but I'll give it a go if you want.'

'It can't make it taste any worse!'

'Actually, it might. Don't blame me if it does.' She reached into her pocket and pulled out a thin piece of crystal about two inches long and pointed at one end.

'Is that a wand?' I asked, intrigued.

'More of a magic channeller. It's kind of a comfort thing – I find it makes me a little more precise in what I'm doing. Jules thinks it's bullshit and she never uses one, but hey.'

'Jules is a witch too?' I said, thinking about all the times I'd met Donna's wife. She was the sort of woman who lit up a room just by stepping into it. I'd always thought that was just her personality, but maybe it was actually her magic. 'I thought you met online.'

'We did, it was an online night for single paras. Now, hold that out for me.' She pointed to the blood bag and closed her eyes.

A peculiar warmth started to fill the car. As I watched with a mixture of disbelief and awe, the crystal started to glow. It wasn't bright like a torch, more like a fading glowstick that was holding on to the last dregs of its power days after a festival had ended. There was nothing chemical about this colour, though: it was like looking at the softest starlight, the gentlest reflection of the moon.

For a moment I assumed that the delicate muted light of the crystal was the source of the heat but then I realised that Donna was radiating energy. Magic was pouring from every pore. How the hell had I not noticed how magical she was before?

A light hum rolled from her throat and warmth continued to spread through the car – until suddenly it was gone. Her eyes pinged open and she pocketed the wand. 'Okay,' she said. 'I'm not sure if that will work because it's not something I've done before. But you've got to drink it.'

I looked at the bag. It didn't look any different. What had I expected? A pineapple-coloured concoction in place of the haemoglobin filled specimen in my hand? Yes, that was exactly what I'd been hoping for.

I sighed. I'd just have to close my eyes and give it a go. I started with a tiny mouthful, then a slightly larger one. 'Okay, it's not piña colada – or at least not an alcoholic one – but it's certainly got a pineapple tang to it.'

'Drink it all quickly,' Donna said. 'I've no idea how long that spell will last, but I'm guessing a couple of minutes at most. I'm not sure it'll work a second time, and the blood might taste even worse afterwards.'

That was all the impetus I needed. Knowing that any second I might have to gulp back viscous, iron-flavoured O-negative, I downed the lot. When I was done, the grin on Donna's face was close to a smirk.

'That spell wasn't going to wear off, was it?' I said, realising I'd been conned.

'No, but I knew you'd just have a tiny drop and tell me some rubbish about being full. Feel better now?'

Better was an interesting word. I still had no pulse,

though my body felt a little more like my own. It was the other effects that were more interesting. I could hear the metal of the car bonnet creaking as it cooled, and the way I was sitting felt slightly at an angle even though the road we were parked on was completely flat.

'I think one of your tyres needs pumping up,' I said. 'Back left. And there's a motorbike going way too fast about to come around the corner.' Before Donna could respond, it whizzed into view.

'Impressive,' she murmured.

'That's nothing,' I said. 'I think I can hear the people in the flat on the fifth floor having an argument about her leaving her underwear next to the laundry basket and not actually putting it inside.' I pointed across the street. 'And there's a woman in that house there who's still reading. I swear I just heard her mutter "one more chapter". There's no way she'll be in a fit state for work tomorrow.'

Or maybe she would be. These new powers of mine were good but I doubted they went as far as predictions and premonitions.

Donna shot me a smile, though it faded quickly. 'It'll be okay, you know. It'll take some adjusting, but you'll be fine.'

'Yeah.' I was actually starting to believe her. 'I just hope Andy feels the same.'

'If he truly loves you, he'll be happy you came back to him and that he didn't lose you for good.'

I forced a smile, grateful that Donna couldn't see the dense knot that was tightening behind my sternum.

CHAPTER
THIRTEEN

We'd been sitting outside the flat for about ten minutes when I heard a familiar noise. 'We should go in,' I said. 'Andy's taxi is about to turn onto the road and I don't think this is a conversation we should have in the street.'

'It's amazing how well you can hear – and that you know it's him.' Donna's eyes widened. 'Is he talking or can you sense other things? You know, his smell or something.'

'His *smell*?' God, hearing things so clearly was one thing – there was no way I wanted to deal with an enhanced sense of smell.

My nose immediately went into overdrive as soon as Donna mentioned it. Wilbur didn't just smell of wet dog, he smelled of a wet dog who'd trampled through a deciduous forest and trodden in rabbit droppings. Donna's overpowering car fresheners were only going part way to cancelling the aromas of the pungent crisps she liked to indulge in – pickled onion, prawn cocktail. What on earth was wrong with good old salt and vinegar?

It seemed that every good thing about being a vampire had a shitty trade-off. Live forever – drink blood. Run super-fast – but only at night when there's no moonlight. Hear for miles – smell the contents of your neighbour's rubbish bin.

I tried to push my new power aside. 'No, I can hear him talking. Sort of.'

Whingeing would be a more accurate description. Apparently, the taxi driver was *deliberately* going over the potholes just to annoy Andy and aggravate his sciatica, something I hadn't even known he suffered from. I was almost certain he'd made it up just so he could be more irate. At that moment Andy was taking down the driver's number so he could make a formal complaint.

To give the driver his due, he sounded incredibly calm when he explained that potholes were beyond his control and no driver would knowingly go over them considering the damage they did to a vehicle. But if Andy wanted to make a complaint, he should go ahead because it might make the council fill them in more quickly.

Suddenly aware that the time I'd been listening had given Andy the opportunity to get closer, I grabbed the door handle. 'We need to get inside now,' I said.

As I opened my door, the first person to jump out was Wilbur. 'Crap,' I swore under my breath.

My heart sank as I looked down at the dog. There was no chance I'd leave him in the car so he had to come inside, but from all the hours he'd spent sitting under my desk at work I knew how quickly he shed his fur. I'd have to get the place deep-cleaned and hope Andy's allergies didn't flare up too badly.

'Okay, boy,' I said as I bounded up the stairs and let Wilbur into the living room. 'If you could find somewhere a bit hidden to stay for a minute, that would be great.'

Wilbur immediately jumped onto Andy's armchair and rolled on his back to deposit as much fur as possible on the cushion. 'No, boy. I'm sorry,' I said, putting him back on the carpet. 'Not on the seat.'

He looked up at me with wide eyes then slunk back onto the chair, curled into a small ball and promptly fell asleep. It wasn't ideal, but at least he wasn't immediately visible.

Donna was looking out of the window. 'Andy's paying the cab. You know, you were seriously fast coming up those stairs. So how do you want to deal with this? Do you want to talk first or do you want me to?'

I had no idea. I was sure Donna was more experienced in this sort of thing so I was happy to let her decide, but before I could say as much I heard the sound of the key sliding into the lock. Three steps later, and Andy was closing the door behind him. '

'Elodie, I'm back. I assume you're awake and that's why the living room light is still on. Honestly, I don't know why you don't just put a lamp on. Well, I hope your night's been better than mine. Half these CEOs have got their priorities completely wrong. Of course I didn't tell them that, but it was £28 for fish and chips! How can they get away with that? And it wasn't even *good* fish and chips. It wasn't fresh oil. And as for the mushy peas, they put mint in them. Mint?'

He was still ranting as he walked into the room and saw Donna and me sitting on the sofa. 'Oh. Donna,' he said. 'What's—? Is everything okay? Wasn't expecting you tonight. Did you come round for a drink?'

His eyes scanned the space for empty wine bottles or glasses and I inhaled sharply as his eyes skipped over his chair. The last thing I need was for him to discover Wilbur before we'd had the vampire conversation. Unless I convinced him that Wilbur was the reason I was still alive – ish. Yes, maybe that would be the best way to approach it.

'No, Donna's here to talk to us about some things,' I said, aware of the tremble in my voice.

'She's not sacking you, is she?' He laughed as he moved towards his chair. I wasn't sure whether vampires needed to breathe or not, but not a single molecule of air entered my lungs as he sat down with his feet only inches from Wilbur's nose.

With a loud yawn, he stretched out his arms, then lay back right where Wilbur had rubbed his fur. 'If so, I hope you get good redundancy. You've still got to cover half the rent.' His tone was only half-joking and it set my nerves on edge.

'No, it's not that,' I said, aware that he was expecting me to offer a reciprocal chuckle. All I managed was a slight smile. 'In fact, Donna's already said I can keep my job so that's not a problem. Although ... there'll have to be some changes.'

He frowned at me. 'Changes? Why? What are you talking about, Elodie.'

This time I took a deep breath in. 'Because something's happened, Andy. To me.'

His face paled. 'What do you mean? What happened? Hang on...' He stared at me, his jaw turning slack. 'You're not pregnant, are you? Oh, my God. You can't be! That isn't something we accounted for at all.'

Had he not already been sitting down, I'm pretty sure he would have toppled to the floor. Instead, he gripped the arms of the chair. 'Babies are messy. So messy. There's the milk and the sick and the nappies—'

'No, Andy, I'm not pregnant.'

He was swaying now. 'I've never seen myself as a—'

'For God's sake, Andy, will you shut up and let someone else speak?' Donna snapped.

Andy's eyes widened. He raised a hand – that I was certain had at least one of Wilbur's hairs on it – and wiped his brow. 'You could have just said that straight away,' he muttered grouchily.

'She probably would have done if you'd let her speak. Now, Elodie has something to tell you.' Donna's eyes locked on mine and I knew exactly what she was saying; she was there and she'd step in at any point if I needed her to.

'Fine. Fine, but I have to say that whatever it is there's no need to be so dramatic. This *is* my home, Donna.'

I gritted my teeth and tried to ignore that he hadn't said *our* home. As he'd already pointed out, I paid for half of everything. Still, I remembered what Donna said about emotions running a little higher after a turning.

I took a deep breath. 'Something happened to me tonight, Andy. I went on a stakeout, even though Donna had told me not to. And I saw some things there... I thought I was helping. But now—'

'Are you in trouble with the law?' His hand flew to his mouth and he leapt to his feet. 'I can't be engaged to a criminal, not with my job. Oh God, am I going to be pulled in for questioning? Will the police think I'm an accessory?' His voice rose.

'Andy, will you just listen?' I snapped. 'This isn't to do with you, it's to do with me. I went on a stakeout and I got bitten. I got bitten by a vampire. I was turned into a *vampire*.'

For the third time in as many minutes, his mouth hung so far open that I could see all the way down to his tonsils. With vampire vision, it really wasn't a pleasant sight; in fact, there were an awful lot of white bumps on them that didn't look healthy. I probably needed tell him about them at some point, once we'd got through this conversation.

Andy continued to stare at me as silence filled the room. I could hear how hard his heart was thudding and I didn't know if he was going to pass out, start yelling, or do something else entirely.

He did none of those things. Instead, he burst out laughing.

'You're joking, right?' He laughed again, more loudly.

'Oh my God, you *really* got me there. A vampire? You do pick your times to try to be funny, Elodie.'

'This isn't a joke, Andy,' Donna snapped.

'And to think I was actually worried!'

'Andy, I need you to believe me,' I warned him.

'Of all the ridiculous things! A vampire!' He wasn't listening; he was too busy wiping away his tears of laughter, ignoring everything Donna and I were trying to tell him.

So I did the only thing I could think of: I took a step towards him and pushed out my fangs.

CHAPTER FOURTEEN

It was strange to actually hear the pace of someone's pulse change – although for a moment Andy's didn't so much change as stop altogether. He was still smiling, but it was like he hadn't chosen to, more that his face had simply frozen in a smile. If it hadn't been for the blood I could hear moving through his body, I could have easily believed that my new state somehow included Gorgon powers and I'd turned his flesh into stone. But no, that wasn't the case.

'Andy.' Donna stood up and reached out a hand. 'This is something we need to talk about.'

Only then did he flinch. He jerked backwards and knocked against the armchair with enough force to wake Wilbur. With an irritated bark, the dog crawled out from underneath it and promptly jumped back into his original spot on the seat.

'Oh my God, there's a dog! A dog in my home. My allergies! My allergies!'

No longer knowing where to direct his panic, Andy sneezed, coughed and wheezed until his eyes locked on the door. He was going to bolt, bolt without understanding that I was still *me*. That everything was still okay.

Before he could take a step, I was there in front of him. His squeal was something I'd have expected to hear in the playground of an all-girls' kindergarten rather than a grown man.

'This is a nightmare,' he said. 'I'm in a nightmare. I have to be.' He took his fingers, pinched the top of his arm and winced.

'Andy, stop it! Please, just listen.'

'Andy.' Donna's voice was low and calm. 'Sit down. Now. Before I make you.' I had heard her sound threatening at work, but her tone had a whole different meaning when you knew she had magic.

Finally, Andy's panic lessened to the point where he could look at her. 'Are you one of them too? Did you do this to her?'

'No, I'm not, but I do know about them. That's why I came here, so I could talk to you and Elodie together and you can understand some of the things that will happen. I can help you adjust to the new way of life.'

Andy's urge to bolt seemed to have faded. Now he was shaking his head so rapidly that his hair was whipping from side to side. 'No. No, I don't want this. This isn't right – it isn't *right*.'

'Andy, it's still me,' I said.

Easy as it had been to push out my fangs, retracting

them was proving a whole lot trickier. Instead, I was making a strange sucking noise that sounded like I was trying to drink blood. It was horrendous and there was nothing I could do to stop it. In the end, I stopped trying to pull in my fangs and spoke around them instead

'It'll be fine, Andy, I promise. It will just take me a little time to get used to it. There are people who actually *want* to become vampires. It doesn't have to be a bad thing.' I reached for his hands but he recoiled and shook his head again.

'No. No, I'm not doing this. This is wrong. Everything about this is wrong.'

'This is me, Andy. Your love. I'm your Elodie. I'm *still* your Elodie.'

As the words left my lips, I heard the desperation in them. Andy wanted to spend his life with me; that was what the ring on my finger meant. Why should that change just because I didn't have a pulse? And yet, as his gaze narrowed and he peered down his nose at me, I knew it had.

'You're a *monster*,' he said. 'You're dead to me and I never want to see you again. Get out – get out before I call the police.'

I felt a crack tear at my non-beating heart. 'Andy, I know this is a huge shock—'

'Get out!'

'This is my home, too!'

His jaw was rigid and a vein on his forehead was throbbing.

Donna had probably been right about drinking the

blood before I came in, though if I bit Andy it wouldn't be because I needed to feed. It would be because I was absolutely furious. Furious that I'd put my faith and trust and love in this man; furious that he would speak to me this way.

I tried one last time. 'Andy, please—' but he wasn't having any of it.

'Get out before I call the police. Or MI5. I'll call—'

I never found out who else he was planning to call because he stopped mid-sentence. His lips were open as he started to form a word but he had frozen again.

It took me a moment to realise why: he had no heartbeat.

I turned and saw Donna standing there, the crystal wand in her hand. 'Oh God! Is he dead?' My panic reached a whole new level.

She shook her head and scowled. 'Nah, though I'm not saying it didn't cross my mind. He's in a time hold, that's all.'

'A time hold?'

'Yes,' she said, 'because that's what we need right now – a bit of time to make a couple of big decisions. It's crunch time, Elodie.'

It wasn't just a case of not *wanting* to make big decisions – I didn't think I was capable of them. Every decision I'd made that night had been wrong; I'd have been better off playing rock-paper-scissors or eenie-meanie-miny-mo.

CHAPTER FIFTEEN

It seemed that the only sound in the room was Wilbur's soft snoring, or maybe that was the only sound I wanted to listen to as I stared at my frozen fiancé.

He *was* my fiancé, wasn't he? No, I didn't think I could call him that now he'd told me he didn't love me and that I was as good as dead to him. Although I was dead, so I couldn't really disagree with that.

Perhaps I should have found a better way of telling him, made it less of a surprise, though I wasn't sure how. A PowerPoint presentation, perhaps? That might have been more up his street.

'He'll just take a little time to accept it,' I said eventually.

'Do you really believe that?' Donna asked. 'This is the man who couldn't accept the fact that they changed the *Bake Off* channel, and who gets annoyed if you put the loo roll the wrong way on the holder. Do you really think he'll get used to you being a vampire?'

I wasn't sure how Donna knew that Andy insisted the loose end of the paper went over and not under the roll, but I knew she was right. Of course he wouldn't get used to me being a vampire.

Andy did everything he could to fight change; half the time, he didn't even like me talking about my job because it made him feel nervous. There was no chance he'd want a life surrounded by werewolves and witches. How the hell had I ever thought he would?

'So what do I do now?' I asked.

Donna shrugged. 'Well, that's up to you.'

I felt a tear escape down my cheek but I hardly dare wipe it away. Didn't vampires cry blood? The impulse to touch my face was too strong to resist, but thankfully it was just a normal tear.

'I know you've said I can have a normal life, but how can I? I'm trapped. I can't even go out in daytime.'

'There are wards to help with that,' she said gently.

'I can't go out for meals with my friends.'

'Sure you can, you just have to drink blood first.'

'I can't have children. I can't travel. There are so many things I *can't* do.'

Donna nodded. 'The children thing is tough, I get that. But as for travelling, there are magical communities all over the world. I've got a good friend who's an editor at a para community on an island near California.'

'You *have*?' I sniffed loudly.

'Yes. I'm pretty sure I can get you a job there, if you like. It's hardly investigative journalism, but—'

'Yes,' I said before I could stop myself. I needed to get

away from here, from Andy and the life I'd expected to have. The thought of bumping into him on the street was enough to make me feel nauseous and, given our cream carpets and my last meal, I really didn't want that to happen.

Donna raised an eyebrow. 'Yes?'

I looked at frozen Andy. My life had changed irrevocably – so why not go the whole hog and move countries as well? It would mean leaving my Dad, but to be honest with all the time I spent working and he spent on holiday with my step-mum, we were lucky if we saw each other three times a year. Still, I half-expected Donna to put up some opposition, to say that I was running away, that I still had a life and a job I loved in London, or that she'd meant the comment flippantly.

She didn't. 'I think that could be a good option for you,' she said. 'A fresh start. And if you decide at some point that you want to come back, you know I'll always have a place for you.'

How was it that I could feel my pulse racing even though I knew I didn't have one? The dryness in my throat was as human a nervous response as any I'd ever had before. Maybe even more so. 'Okay,' I said. 'You can sort it out?'

'Yes,' she promised. 'In fact, you going there might actually help me out. I was worried I'd have to take some time off work because I have something that needs dropping off on route. It's not something that I'd trust most people to look after.'

'Which is?' I asked. I had to hand it to Donna: she

knew that the best way to mend my broken heart was to tease me with work.

She rolled her eyes. ‘A basilisk egg.’

‘A what?’

‘Don’t ask. It was found in a smuggling raid a couple of months ago. You can drop it off en route.’

Dropping off a basilisk egg en route to Los Angeles? Where the hell did you leave something like that?

I couldn’t imagine a version of my old life where I’d get to do something like that, but I was quickly learning that the world was now a very different place. ‘What do I do about him?’ I nodded at Andy.

‘Oh, quick memory wipe, just like Linda and Marcus. We can tell him you’ve got a new job abroad and he didn’t want to come with you, so you ended your engagement.’

‘Yeah.’ The word came out more feebly than I’d anticipated, so I cleared my throat and tried again. ‘Yeah. That sounds good.’ I tried to quash the sadness that came with ending my relationship with a lie, but I’d tried the truth and that was how we’d ended up here.

‘Shall we get your things?’ Donna said. ‘The spell has got about another twenty minutes. It’s really not safe to leave it on him any longer than that.’

‘Twenty minutes is fine,’ I said.

Wilbur was still asleep on the chair and I was damned if I was cleaning up a single one of his hairs. Screw Andy. He didn’t love me. In fact, I hoped he inhaled a dog hair and choked on it, or at least got a nasty rash. I didn’t really want him to die; I wanted him to live long enough to realise that he’d made a huge mistake in letting me go.

'I can pack your clothes if you want, while you collect everything else you need,' Donna said.

'Actually there's something else I'd like you to do.' The idea had fluttered into my mind when I'd looked at Wilbur and I couldn't stop the grin curling my lips. Yes, it was wrong and petty, but I didn't care. After the way Andy had just broken my heart, I deserved a bit of petty – and he deserved every bit of bad karma that came his way. Besides, it would be for a good cause.

'Sure,' Donna replied.

I disappeared into the bedroom then returned a moment later with a stack of envelopes and a pen. I put them on the dining table before walking over to Andy, putting my hand in his pocket and pulling out his wallet.

I threw it to Donna then pointed at the envelopes. 'Those are animal charities – and they're all about to get a lovely donation.'

She grinned back at me. 'Elodie Evergreen, I wouldn't have thought you had it in you.'

'Well, I think we're going to see a slightly different version of me from now on,' I said. A flutter of excitement was building within me. 'A new, vampire, California-based Elodie Evergreen.'

'California-based Elodie Evergreen.' Her smile faltered and a look of panic flashed across her eyes. 'My best friend is going to be on the other side of the world. Maybe this isn't such a good idea after all.'

I wasn't immune to the same fear but what choice did I have? My life here was over. 'Of course it is.'

I took her hands and was about to squeeze them, but

then I stopped. I had no idea how strong I was and the last thing I wanted to give Donna as a parting gift was broken knuckles and fractured fingers. 'I'll be ringing you all the time. You'll need to keep me up to date on how everything is going at the paper.'

The smile she offered me was watery and weak. 'I'll miss you, but you're going to love it. You show the journalists over there what you're made of.'

'Oh, don't worry. I will. This new Elodie Evergreen is going to bring it on.'

IF YOU HAVE ENJOYED Elodie's adventure, be sure to see follow her to Ravens Hollow in this thrilling new series to find out what new trouble her journalistic skills will land her in next.

FANGS AND FRONTPAGES

A RAVENS HOLLOW INVESTIGATION

The scoop of a lifetime, or something far deadlier?

Starting over was meant to be simple - a chance to adjust to my new, nocturnal existence. No men. No complications. Just a bit of light investigative journalism in a quaint magical town by the sea.

Then Pongo the pup trotted into my life, and normalcy bled away faster than my resistance to a fresh pint of blood. I'd barely set up my desk at the Ravens Hollow Oracle before a renowned sculptor turned up dead at the town's annual art exhibition.

What better way to get to know a place than by investigating its most suspicious residents? The only snag was Chief Whip - the infuriatingly handsome local lawman who'd rather I kept my fangs and my nose out of his murder investigation.

Too bad. The body count is rising, and whether he likes it or not, he needs me. My instincts are razor-sharp. My fangs? Even sharper.

NOTE FROM ELLA

First off, thank you for taking the time to read **Bylines and Bloodsuckers**, a prequel to the Ravens Hollow Investigations Series. If you enjoyed the book, I'd love for you to let your friends know so they can also experience this action-packed adventure. I have enabled the lending feature where possible, so it is easy to share with a friend.

If you leave a review **Bylines and Bloodsuckers** on Amazon, Goodreads, Bookbub, or even your own blog or social media, I would love to read it. You can email me the link at ella@ellastoneauthor.com

Don't forget, you can stay up-to-date on upcoming releases and sales by joining my newsletter, following my social media pages or visiting my website www.ellastoneauthor.com

About the Author

I am an author of Urban Fantasy and Paranormal Fiction. I'm passionate about my family, reading, writing and cats. The order of which can change on a day to day basis.

Printed in Dunstable, United Kingdom

68973695R00060